# DOCTOR WHO

# THE ZYGON INVASION

# DOCTOR WHO

# THE ZYGON INVASION

Based on the BBC television adventures
'The Zygon Invasion' and 'The Zygon Inversion'
by Peter Harness and Steven Moffat

PETER HARNESS

1

BBC Books, an imprint of Ebury Publishing
20 Vauxhall Bridge Road
London SW1V 2SA

BBC Books is part of the Penguin Random House group of companies
whose addresses can be found at global.penguinrandomhouse.com

Doctor Who is produced in Wales by Bad Wolf with BBC Studios Productions.

Executive Producers: Russell T Davies, Julie Gardner, Jane Tranter, Phil Collinson & Joel Collins

First published by BBC Books in 2023

www.penguin.co.uk

A CIP catalogue record for this book is available from the British Library

ISBN 9781785947919

Typeset in 11.4/14.6pt Adobe Caslon Pro by Jouve (UK), Milton Keynes
Printed and bound in Great Britain by Clays Ltd, Elcograf S.p.A.

The authorised representative in the EEA is Penguin Random House Ireland, Morrison Chambers, 32 Nassau Street, Dublin D02 YH68

*To my beloved mum and dad, Marion and Ted,*
*with love and thanks for a happy childhood*
*full of Target books*

# Contents

# Prologue

*It was a choice made by someone else.*

*'Fit in,' that was what they said. 'It's vital that you try to fit in.'*

*But she didn't want to fit in. She wanted to be herself.*

'Any second now,' said the Doctor with the sandshoes, 'you're going to stop that countdown. Both of you. Together.'

The urgent red numbers on the clock stood at 00:51. Slightly less than a minute.

'And then,' said the slightly younger-looking Doctor with the waistcoat, 'you're going to negotiate the most perfect peace treaty of all time.'

'Safeguards all round,' interrupted the Doctor with the sandshoes. 'Completely fair on both sides.'

The other Doctor, the third one in the room – the old one with the beard who had never really thought of himself as 'the Doctor' until now – watched them: a smile beginning to break across the sad lines of his face, like longed-for rainwater through a dried-up riverbed.

'And the key to perfect negotiation—' said Waistcoat—

'Is not knowing what side you're on!' said Sandshoes.

With that, Sandshoes and Waistcoat kicked their long legs against the table, slid back their chairs, and, with a theatrical flourish, got to their feet. Two Doctors, at the height of their power. Doing what they did best: improvising.

'So for the next two hours—' said Sandshoes—

'Until we decide to let you out—' said Waistcoat—

'No one in this room will be able to remember if they're human—'

'—or Zygon.'

The Doctors brandished their sonic screwdrivers and jumped onto the table, one of them rather undermining the intensity of the moment by shouting out the old action hero standby, 'Oops-a-daisy!'

They aimed their screwdrivers at a small device, looking something like a smoke detector, concealed quietly in the ceiling of the room. It clearly wasn't a smoke detector, however, as it failed to detect itself as it glowed brighter and brighter, and emitted a gigantic belch of mind-altering gas.

The old Doctor – the wrinkled, battered version with the voice that seemed to have been tuned and broken in the tumult of the battlefield – took out his sonic screwdriver too and joined in with the boys. All of a sudden, he felt more optimistic than he had been in centuries: ready once more to be a joiner-in. Let the device have it, whatever it was.

For a moment, everything in the room was dazzling light. The gas filled the air. Everyone inhaled. And everyone who was not the Doctor fell asleep. And everyone who was not the Doctor lost their memory of who they were.*

Moments later, the people woke up.

The urgent red countdown clock stood at 00.08.

00.07 – 00.06 –

'Cancel the detonation!' cried two panicked voices, in perfect unison.

The clock stopped. 00.05.

The two panicked voices belonged to two women called Kate Lethbridge-Stewart (although known professionally as plain Kate Stewart). Besides the Kates and the Doctors (who had just shouted out 'Peace in Our Time!'), there were three other people in the room: one was a woman in her twenties called Clara Oswald, who travelled with the Waistcoat Doctor when she felt like it. The other two were a young scientist called Osgood and another young scientist called Osgood. One of the Kates Stewart was an alien duplicate as was

---

* See DOCTOR WHO – THE DAY OF THE DOCTOR

one of the Osgoods. A living facsimile, perfect in every respect: a Zygon.

The room was called the Black Archive. It was a repository for the most secret and dangerous alien technology that had been collected over the years: a place for things which should not be on Earth but which somehow were. Even its own staff were not allowed to know what it held. They had their memories wiped after every shift: something that the people who worked in the Black Archive always meant to raise with Human Resources but never remembered to do. Above the room was the Tower of London, and beneath the room was a nuclear bomb.

Over the next two hours, Kate Stewart and Kate Stewart – ignorant, as the Doctors suggested, of which side they were on – negotiated the so-called 'perfect peace treaty'. The Zygons – a race of creatures who could borrow the forms of other creatures, whose home planet had been destroyed in the war in which the older Doctor had lost his name, amongst other things – were in the middle of mounting an invasion. The invasion was to stop but the Zygons were to be allowed to remain on Earth. They were to take human form and stay that way. Kate Stewart and Osgood were to support and assist them in their new life. In exchange for this, the Zygons were to call off their attempt to take over planet Earth and generally do their best to fit in. As the Doctors instructed, Kate and Kate and Osgood and Osgood built in safeguards, fairness. They tried to imagine the ways in which this scenario could play out and how the ceasefire could be maintained. It was the very best that they could do in the scant few hours that they were given.

And after the papers were all signed and hands were shaken, the humans and the Zygons regained their knowledge of which was which and who was who. The Doctors moved on to other business elsewhere; the picking up of the pieces started, and the peace began in earnest. For the Doctors, centuries passed. On Earth, it was more like a couple of years.

But nothing is ever perfect.

There is never an easy solution to a difficult problem.

Soon enough, those same people would find themselves back in that same room. Trying to solve the very same problem.

Only this time they would know exactly who was who.

# Chapter 1

## Operation Double

Osgood set up a camera to record their message. They wore a tank-top with question marks on it under a white lab coat. They were in the basement of a safe-house in South West London, operated by UNIT: the Unified Intelligence Taskforce.

Osgood had been UNIT's scientific adviser for some time. It ran in the family: their father had done pretty much the same job in the seventies or eighties too. He had always seemed to have an exciting time; he had retired at fifty with a bionic eye and a decent pension; Osgood had always wanted to be like their father, so they had put in their application and been approved. Osgood worked alongside Kate Stewart, the Chief Scientific Officer, whose father had also worked for UNIT back in the day. If UNIT had been remotely public-facing, or in the least bit accountable, there would surely have been eyebrows raised about the level of nepotism that seemed to be permissible there. But it seemed to work, more or less. Nobody asked too many questions.

Another thing about which UNIT managed to keep successfully quiet was the existence of their *former* scientific adviser: the mysterious traveller in time and space known as the Doctor. Osgood had met him once at a UNIT picnic when they were still a child. At that time, he had been dressed like a refugee from one of the sixties TV shows that used to be repeated at teatimes on BBC Two: all velvet jackets and frills. He did a little magic show for the little Osgood that kept them enchanted. He had introduced them to gorgonzola cheese. That version of the Doctor disappeared some time later, to be replaced by another with a long scarf and curly hair, who was even more intriguing. Osgood had kept tabs on him over the years and had become quite a fan.

Another Osgood came into the room and sat beside the Osgood who was already there. This Osgood wore a multi-coloured scarf similar to one that the curly-haired Doctor used to sport.

'Do you want to start?' said Osgood.

'No, you can,' said Osgood.

Osgood was just getting to know themselves. They thought that the best way to ensure that things went well between them was to be excessively polite and apologise to one another as much as possible. One was a human and the other was a Zygon. To begin with, they had some idea of who was who and which was which, but the more the two Osgoods lived together, the more the line became blurred; the more they forgot themselves.

After the shakedown in the Black Archive, the Zygon doubles of Kate Stewart and various others around the world had vacated their stolen forms and become different. But the Osgoods had stayed the same. The Doctors felt this was important to maintain the ceasefire: there should be a living symbol of the peace: someone who could be an honest broker, with no agenda, able to move between the various sides and factions, with a knowledge of what it was like to be a human, and what it was like to be a Zygon.

To begin with, Osgood had found it rather intrusive: perpetually having a doppelganger mooching around, reminding themself of all their blemishes; confronting themself all the time with the way that they looked and breathed and hunched their shoulders. But, to be honest, Osgood had always been rather lacking in the friends department, feeling something of an outsider. And there turned out to be something about their other self that they rather liked. They shared a small two-bedroom flat in Stockwell, just off the South Lambeth Road. Both Osgoods were paid a decent salary for doing the same job and they only had to do half the work that they used to. In their spare time, they had taken up badminton.

'Shall we do it together?'

They turned to the camera.

'Hello,' they said.

'Operation Double – The Zygon Peace Treaty,' they said in unison, adjusting their glasses.

'I am Osgood,' said the one with the tank-top.

'I am also Osgood,' said the one with the scarf. 'Remember that. It'll be important later.'

'Operation Double is a covert operation,' said the first, getting down to business. 'Outside of normal UNIT strictures. To resettle and rehouse an alien race, in secrecy, on planet Earth.'

'With UNIT's help,' continued the second, clearing their throat, 'twenty million Zygons have been allowed to take human form, have been dispersed around the world, and are now living amongst us. They're living peacefully, usefully. But they're doing this without the knowledge of any of Earth's authorities.'

Both Osgoods coloured up a little: 'In most countries,' said the first, 'what we've done would be considered treason. At the very least, it's an alien invasion . . . So. Sorry for that. But it was probably better than the alternative.'

'We're making this recording in case something goes wrong,' said the second. 'In case UNIT is infiltrated. In case something occurs to unmask the Zygons.'

'Or in case one or both of us dies.'

There was something rather ominous about this

last sentence, and each Osgood felt a shudder of premonition run through their body; as if someone had just walked across their grave.

'The Zygons are a peaceful race,' continued Osgood. 'Their shape-changing abilities should not be considered a weapon. It's a survival mechanism.'

'They embed themselves in other cultures. Live out their lives in their new bodies. In peace and harmony. Mainly.'

'But any race is capable of the best and the worst.'

'Every race is peaceful and warlike. Good and evil.'

'My race is no exception,' said the Zygon Osgood.

'And neither is mine,' said the human.

They reached forward and put their hand on a blue wooden box sitting on the table in front of them.

'That's why the Doctor left us this,' they said, their voice skipping a little with excitement at the name of their hero. 'He called it the Osgood Box,' they said, with some pride. 'If you've been paying attention, you'll be able to guess why.'

The box was covered in carved symbols. It clearly contained something important. There had been a similar box kicking around on that decisive day in the Black Archive. A similar box that the Doctor had used to solve a similar problem.

'This is the last resort,' continued Osgood. 'The final sanction. Pray that this box is never needed . . .'

'. . . Because if it is, that means the ceasefire has been

breached and we're on the verge of war. And with twenty million shape-changing Zygons dispersed around the world ...'

'That is the nightmare scenario.'

A few months after the Osgoods sat in the basement of the UNIT safehouse and left their recording, one of them did indeed die. That Osgood was vaporised by Missy – an enemy of the Doctor's, known previously as the Master. The other Osgood was alone again.

But it was harder than they could have possibly imagined. The loss of a person who had very quickly become their closest friend, their twin – a person who shared all their experiences, feelings and memories – was painful enough in itself. But the severing of such a primal link between two people who have more or less become the same, who have begun to live in one another's bodies and one another's minds, was almost unbearable. Osgood found it very hard to recover. But they had to, because there was business to take care of.

And things were starting to deteriorate.

Six months after the video recording had been made, guns were firing. Explosions blew dust from the sandy streets up into the hot desert air. It was choking. Terrifying. The middle of a warzone, in the midst of a firefight, is one of the most intense and incredible situations that a person can find themselves in. Death, cordite and electricity.

Osgood – the sole surviving Osgood – ran across the square to a police station in a white-plastered building which looked like an ancient hacienda. They were in a town called Truth or Consequences. It was in New Mexico, in the United States of America.

Osgood dodged a screaming hail of bullets. A man with a bloodied face staggered past. Perhaps he was human. Perhaps he was a Zygon. But Osgood could not stop to help, either way: they needed to make a call. The terms of the peace settlement had been comprehensively breached and the situation was out of control.

Inside the station, Osgood looked desperately around for help, advice or assistance. But none was obtainable and it looked like all the police in this particular box were either dead or missing.

Another explosion, much nearer, blew through the windows and scattered stones and sand across the room. The enemy was closing in. Time was limited.

Osgood crouched under a desk in the office of the station commander, squared their back to the wall, and took out their inhaler. The blast of steroids cleared their lungs and their head. They brought their phone close, squinting at it through the broken lenses of their glasses and found the contact they were looking for. Osgood made a prayer that they had reception, that their phone wasn't damaged. That he would answer.

Then everything stopped.

Something was in the room with them.

Something breathing with a wheezing, unnatural sound. The sound of a creature unused to the atmosphere of Earth. The sound of a Zygon, in its natural form.

*They shouldn't be in their natural form*, thought Osgood to themself. *Why are they doing this?*

Heavy footsteps sounded across the floor. Osgood peered out: two reddish green feet stomped across the dust and broken glass. Paused.

Osgood knew they were being hunted. Scented. They hoped the smell of death in the air would mask the scent of fear.

They took up the phone and, with trembling hands, tried to type out a message as best they could. They looked around the whole time, wishing the sound of breathing and the heavy footsteps would take a different turn. Osgood could sense the creature's mind reaching out for them. Fishing for the tick of brain chemicals; listening for the beat of a heart.

Osgood typed the message, cursing autocorrect and the sweat on their fingers. Then they looked up. The footsteps had gone. The room was silent. Had the hunter moved away?

Osgood leaned slightly forward, peered out from beneath the table. Moving as slowly and as softly as they possibly could.

And a claw snatched them. Grabbed their neck. Dragged them violently out from their hiding place.

The Zygon sneered, baring piranha-like teeth, and raised its hand to Osgood's temples.

A crackling bolt of electricity shot right through their brain: the sting of the Zygon. Osgood crumpled into oblivion. Their hand let go of the phone and it clattered to the floor.

The last surviving Osgood. Gone dark.

In the TARDIS, the Doctor was playing his guitar. 'Amazing Grace', in the style of one of his former travelling companions, Jimi Hendrix. This Doctor was tall and thin, with a shock of grey hair and deep blue eyes beneath fierce brows. He sounded Scottish but preferred to think of himself as Gallifregian.

The screen on the console came to life:

INCOMING MESSAGE
OSGOOD

The Doctor walked towards the screen, the accumulated grimness and gravity of his many thousands of lived years falling across his face. He knew before it came what the message would be.

NIGHTMARE
SCENARIO

# Chapter 2

## The Twins at the Park

*Hi, this is Clara Oswald. I'm probably on the tube. Or in outer space. Leave a message!* BEEP.

'Hello, this is Doctor Disco. I'm in the twenty-first century. Don't know what month. I'm staking out some of the most dangerous creatures imaginable.'

The Doctor paused and watched a primary school teacher lead a crocodile-line of schoolchildren through the empty playground in which he was currently sitting. It was a grey afternoon at the turn of the season from autumn to winter. Brockwell Park, in South London. The TARDIS was parked nearby.

Two small girls with pigtails, identical twins – one with a Cinderella rucksack, the other holding something similar but promoting *Monster High* – stopped at the end of the line and looked coldly over at him. He stared at them from his swing. These were the deadly creatures to which he was referring.

'I'm operating under deep cover,' the Doctor went on into the phone. 'Trying not to attract suspicion.' He got off the swing. 'Give me a call, Clara. Nightmare scenario. I'm worried.'

The Doctor hung up, took off his sunglasses and made for the climbing frame where the pigtailed twins were playing while their teacher was distracted across the park.

'Okay – hey, you – Monster High and Cinderella. Down off the monkey bars. Listen to me, we need to *talk*.'

'Get me Colonel Walsh,' said Kate. And in a lower voice, 'Jac, I need you to coordinate the Operation Double locations.'

Kate Stewart and Jac, her deputy, shuttled down several flights of stairs in a disused house not so far away from where the Doctor was currently 'undercover' in a playground. This was the UNIT safehouse where Osgood had made their tape, and where this most secret of secret plans had been enacted. Jac was bringing up data on her iPad.

'Coordinate the locations? You're talking about twenty million Zygons,' said Jac, harassed and anxious, as they stopped at the door of a room which used to be Osgood's office. 'And most of the data . . .'

Jac's voice tailed off. Most of the data had been with Osgood, and now she was missing in action. Presumed dead.

Kate paused too. There was Osgood's desk, just

across the room. The photo of Osgood's dad, the scarf, the inhaler. The things that meant something to someone who was no longer there.

'Do what you can,' replied Kate, with a catch in her voice. 'Start with any that have had intelligence flags in the last six months.'

Jac followed Kate into the main operational area, passing various UNIT personnel who were busy at their workstations. Jac's iPad screen flashed. Colonel Walsh was coming through. Kate looked up at the video call on the big screen.

'Walsh, Turmezistan,' said a serious-looking woman in a red beret and black military tunic, bearing the ribbons of her many campaigns. She was UNIT's field commander for Central Asia, currently stationed in a distant, desolate country on the edge of the Karakum Desert and the Old Silk Road, recently the site of suspicious activity.

'Any new arrivals?' asked Kate.

'One,' replied Colonel Walsh. 'Picture's not very good.'

Footage from a spy drone broke through on Kate's screen. A black-and-white view of a remote encampment in the mountains on the edge of the west Asian steppe. It could only be a training camp. A training camp for a breakaway Zygon faction.

Kate put on her glasses. Two figures could be seen, leading a third. Only one of them looked human. 'Can you zoom in on the prisoner?'

The image focused in. Clarified. It was Osgood. The others were their Zygon captors.

'It's her,' said Kate.

'Them,' corrected Jac.

'There's one of her now. She's a her,' said Kate impatiently. 'Get into her files. We have to assume they've been compromised. We have to assume that she's been tortured and that she's talked.'

Jac was ahead of her. She was already decrypting Osgood's files. She recoiled from the screen as though some disgusting creature had just crept out from it. Instead of the expected array of intelligence folders and documents, all that could be seen was a rapidly increasing jumble of text, which read:

TRUTH OR CONSEQUENCES TRUTH OR CONSEQUENCES TRUTH OR CONSEQUENCES TRUTH OR CONSEQUENCES

Over and over again.

'Too late,' said Jac. 'The encryption system's already been hacked.'

Kate came to Jac's side. The text faded away and was replaced with a video file. 'And they've sent another tape.'

Jac clicked PLAY.

*

'Look. I admire you, okay?' said the Doctor to the twins in the playground, all the time glancing up to their teacher to check she was still busy. 'I think it's genius. Pretending to be a couple of seven-year-old girls. It's a splendid way to conceal your blobbiness. But let's face it. You are very blobby. In fact, I have reason to believe that you two are the Big Blobs.' ('The Big Blobs' being the technical term for the Zygon High Command on planet Earth.) He came confidentially closer to them and hissed: 'And you are not patrolling the ceasefire.'

The two little girls looked at the Doctor as though he was some sort of insane Scotsman and continued clambering down from the climbing frame.

The Doctor headed them off at the slide. 'Listen!'

They stopped and looked at him.

'There are other factions,' he insisted. 'I know there are other blobby factions that you don't control. They're planning something. And if you and me don't get together and find out what it is, it'll be the end of this. The end of *you*.'

There was silence for a moment. The two girls stood quite still, evaluating him. Their cold seven-year-old eyes sizing him up with calm, dangerous intelligence. Then they spoke.

'This is our jurisdiction, Doctor,' said the first. 'We are close to finding them.'

'These are our children. And we will deal with them,' said the second coolly.

'No,' said the Doctor. 'Your kids are out of control. I'm taking this out of your hands.'

The Doctor's phone rang. *STEWART, KATE*. He turned away to take the call, a few paces out of earshot.

'Don't even think about going anywhere,' he warned over his shoulder.

The twins came down from the climbing frame and took a step towards the seesaw, conferring quietly with one another. Their teacher glanced up and wondered what was going on.

'Are you phoning me with your backside again,' said the Doctor, 'or are you really sending me a distress signal?'

'I'm really sending you a distress signal,' replied Kate. 'They've kidnapped Osgood, and they've stolen the location of every Zygon on Earth. Doctor, the ceasefire's broken down.'

Suddenly, there was a loud thud and a vicious hiss. The Doctor turned. A gnarled, organic-looking grenade had landed right in the middle of the playground. It was belching forth acrid red smoke at terrific speed and in amazing volume. Within half a second, everything was drowning in a red fog. The twins turned, hand-in-hand. Two men in high-visibility tabards were marching towards them.

The Doctor moved into action, eyes widening. He sprinted back towards the twins, yelling, 'Away – get away!' to the other kids who were scattering around, crying and confused. Panicking, the teacher tried to round up the children. The red mist was everywhere. And the twins were at the heart of it.

As he reached the spot where he'd left them moments before, the Doctor could just barely make out, in the flurry of fleeing school uniforms, two sets of legs flailing in the air as the twins were carried off by the men with the hi-vis tabards.

Only they were no longer men. They were Zygons.

The sounds of screaming kids caused the Doctor an almost physical pain. Lungs bursting, he broke through to the other side of the dense red smoke and stopped at the edge of the playground. A green van marked PARKS MAINTENANCE was speeding across the grass verges. A woman pushing her baby in a pram swerved madly out of its way as the van smashed through the fence and screeched off into the London traffic.

The Doctor came to a halt and checked to see that the woman and child were safe. They were fine; only shaken.

But the Doctor was not fine. He'd taken his eye off the ball. He needed to catch up, and he needed to get to UNIT. Fast.

Beside the swings, beside the TARDIS, was a sign, bearing strange graffiti. Something that looked like a trident. Or a three-fingered hand.

A Zygon hand. An emblem. A rallying point. A declaration of war.

The video clip began with a shot of the very same insignia.

Panning down, the image adjusted for the darkness in the room, and focused on Osgood, sitting behind a table. A hostage, reading out a prepared message from their captors. A familiar human technique, now perfectly copied and used by aliens.

'UNIT troops will be destroyed,' Osgood read. 'Wherever they are in the world.'

The light of a naked bulb cast a bleak and pessimistic mood over the plain desk and the bleak script thereon. There were shadows on the wall behind them. Non-human shadows. Watching, intimidating, commanding. The shadows of the captors behind the camera.

Osgood looked up, scared, reluctant. A small moment of defiance: a last ounce of fight.

Whoever was making the video nodded them on.

'The enemies of our race will be destroyed wherever they are in the world.'

Two Zygons stepped into the frame either side of Osgood, flanking them. Within touching distance. Threatening.

Osgood read the final sentence: 'The war . . . is about to begin.' They flinched as one of the Zygons shuffled towards them. 'There will be truth. Or there will be consequences.'

Osgood looked up into the camera. Silently imploring the viewer for help. And then the video clip ended. The three-fingered insignia took its place on screen.

In Kate's office at the UNIT safehouse, the Doctor watched grimly with Kate Stewart and Jac by his side. He knew they were dealing with something new here. Something organised, something innovative. Something with a plan and a dangerous ideology.

The Doctor lifted his phone. He had not heard from Clara for a very long time. She was here, in London. And therefore she was in danger. These creatures had kidnapped Osgood and they seemed to be several steps ahead of the game.

*Hi, this is Clara Oswald. I'm probably on the tube. Or in outer space. Leave a message!* BEEP

'Call-me-*now*,' the Doctor said and hung up angrily.

## Chapter 3

## The Boy on the Stairs

Clara Oswin Oswald, time traveller and schoolteacher, removed her motorcycle helmet and swung herself off her Vespa. The day was bright and pleasant. It felt good to have the wind on her hair. She was wearing a black leather jacket and deep red lipstick.

Clara was twenty-eight years old and, for the past few years, she'd been mixed up with a suspicious gentleman in a blue box who hopped periodically into her life and caused varying degrees of chaos.

Clara had a complicated relationship with chaos. In what she thought of as her everyday life, she was always sure to exercise a tight degree of control. She liked things neat and orderly and became uncomfortable if she wasn't in charge. However, there was a strange and messy and powerful feeling somewhere deep within her. A dangerous feeling – a desire almost – to seek confusion and uncertainty and let herself be borne away by them, like a leaf tumbling on the wind. She thought of this as her 'neveryday' life.

The Doctor, with his box of secrets, seemed to come from that dark and dangerous neveryday within her. She wondered sometimes whether, in fact, she hadn't called him up herself; summoned him, like a demon from the caves of her subconscious mind. The TARDIS, his time machine, seemed to be a perfect expression of her own psyche. On the outside: tidy, authoritative and interesting to look at. On the inside: more vast than imagination, capable of going anywhere, and full of haphazard and dangerous things.

When she felt the breeze in her hair, she felt good.

A couple of years ago, Clara had loved a man called Danny Pink; loved and lost him. He had been her colleague at school, young and good and brave. He'd died in an accident. Danny had been knowable. Secure. He'd felt like a rock to cling to in a wild sea. This was something that she needed, but she had lost him and he was dead.

Since Danny died, Clara found herself clinging on to these brief moments in which some small thing made her feel good. They were important: unexpected islands, stepping stones. The frost on the morning grass. The late autumn sun. That breeze in her hair.

She locked the scooter and walked with a spring towards the entrance hall of her block of flats, taking off her gloves and reaching for her phone.

It beeped.

THE DOCTOR, it said. 127 MISSED CALLS.

Clara laughed to herself. She checked her voicemail, laughed again, turned the corner of her stairs and lifted the phone to call him back.

But suddenly, she stopped dead.

A little boy was sitting there in the darkness between two windows, halfway up the flight of stairs. She knew him. He was called Sandeep. He lived two floors beneath her with his mum and dad.

He glanced up at her. 'Hello,' he murmured plaintively. Something was the matter. She knew him to be a sensitive child. Shy and nervous. But this was more than that. He was unsettled and afraid.

Clara pocketed her phone and gave him an encouraging smile. 'Sandeep, hello! Y'okay?'

The boy started to cry and buried his head in his hands: as heartbroken and worried as only a little boy of eight years can be when something has gone wrong with his little world. 'I can't find Mummy and Daddy,' he said.

Clara looked at him with concern but continued breezily. 'Well, why don't you wait here and I can go see if I can find them?'

Sandeep nodded. Clara smiled back and walked down the corridor to the door of Sandeep's place. This was nothing to worry about, she decided. She was a schoolteacher; she knew how kids worked, and she knew how families worked. Clara could fix it.

But something felt deeply wrong as she stepped

through the half-open front door and into the dim hallway of the little boy's home. Some sudden sensation of evil accosted her like a poltergeist. For a second it felt like she'd walked into another world. Despite the sunshine outside, the flat was dark and cold. And there was a strange, toxic smell of burning in the air. Like burnt toast. No. Like burnt *hair*. Or fingernails . . .

'Hello?' Her voice echoed dully down towards the bedrooms. Was anyone here? She tried the light switch by the door. Nothing. Just dark.

'Hello?' she tried again, and walked on, beginning to wonder what she would do if – as a gnawing feeling at the base of her neck was beginning to tell her – something awful had happened to Sandeep's parents. She began to wonder what she might find when she turned the corner and looked into the bedroom and didn't like the images in her mind.

Clara walked slowly into the first room. The living area with a kitchenette just off. There was no one there. A meal, half-eaten, sat on the table. Maggots were beginning to crawl from it. Nobody had eaten there for a couple of days. Had Sandeep been on his own for that long?

Suddenly, a dark shape moved in the corridor behind her. She turned, drawing a sharp breath, a surge of adrenalin whooshing into her blood.

It was Sandeep's father.

He stood there with a grim expression on his face,

watching her with black, intimidating eyes. He was standing in the doorway. She would have to make her way past him if she needed to get out. He was a big man, and she was alone with him. Clara talked big but she was small physically.

She took a couple of paces back. 'Sorry,' she said, trying to sound normal. 'Your little boy ... is out there ... Sandeep.'

She looked at the man's face for some sort of tic of concern or recognition. None came, and he continued to move slowly towards her. She was beginning to get scared. Her fingers found her housekeys in her pocket. She slotted them between her knuckles, making a secret fist.

'He couldn't find you. He didn't know where you were,' she told him.

The man looked over his shoulder. He shuffled out into the hall. 'Daddy's here,' he said. But there was no warmth or reassurance in his tone.

Clara moved out to follow the man, but found her way blocked by Sandeep's mum. She looked at Clara with the same strange intensity as the man had done. And, although the woman was much smaller, Clara found her just as intimidating.

'Is Sandeep okay?' Clara asked, convinced by now that absolutely nothing here was okay. She didn't know this family well, but they weren't like *this*. They were fun, friendly. Sometimes they kept parcels for her when she was at work. But right now they just seemed *horrible.*

'He's fine,' said the woman, a greasy, toothy leer breaking out over her face. Clara realised that she was trying to smile.

Sandeep was carried into the flat in his father's arms, but he wasn't happy or comforted. He was kicking, screaming. Clara's mind started to run through what she was going to do when she got out of this place, who she could call for help. Every alarm bell in her body was ringing – she had to get Sandeep away from this place.

Clara opened her mouth to say something, but the woman stepped in, saying, 'We've got him now. You should leave.'

And, though her mind was whirling with conflicted feelings, Clara found herself doing so.

She put up her hair as she left the flat. It felt more business-like. More suitable. She took the phone out of her jacket, remembering where she'd left off, and listened to the voicemail again. She called the Doctor. And this time she got through.

'Did you just call yourself "Doctor Disco"?' she asked.

A school in darkness. A haunted place.

In Clara's memory was a distant recollection of a belief that she'd once had that her teachers actually slept at school. That they waved the pupils off at the end of the day and then just curled up in the classrooms and slept under the desks. The memory had returned when she'd begun her teaching career. Clara had often wondered what it would be like to sleep over at school. That was a weird thought. It didn't make any sense. Clara found herself noticing that a lot of the thoughts in her head were weird and made no sense these days.

'This is where the Zygon High Command had their secret base,' said Kate Stewart.

They were in a primary school in Dulwich, South London. It was the same school that the twins – or rather the Zygon High Command – attended. They walked past the photos of the twins, above the hooks where they used to hang their coats and bags. It was a good place to hide, Clara thought. Human beings – on the whole – adored and protected their children above all things. It was an excellent idea to lay your cuckoo's eggs in this particular nest. Clara studied the Doctor, who was walking beside her. He was lost in thought.

'Terms of the settlement, Operation Double,' Kate went on, 'were these. Twenty million Zygons were allowed to be born and to stay on Earth – the entire hatchery. And they were allowed to permanently take on the form of the nearest available human beings.'

'In this case,' added Jac, 'a large percentage of the population of the UK.'

The Doctor grunted. He clearly didn't like the terms of the settlement.

'You know this, Doctor, you were there,' said Kate.

'It was a long time ago. I was three completely different people.'

Kate sighed. 'They were dispersed around the planet, to live normal lives as normal people in out-of-the-way places—'

'And since then?' said the Doctor. 'This is the most important ceasefire in human history, Kate. How have you policed it?'

'You left us with an impossible situation, Doctor.'

Clara remembered that the Doctor tended to do that. Nearly everything about him was fundamentally impossible.

'Yes, I know it was an impossible situation,' said the Doctor casually. 'It's called "peace".'

'No, Doctor,' said Kate. 'It's called you instructing us to do something so complicated as to be almost unachievable and then clearing off before you've sorted out the details.'

They arrived at a boiler room in the cellars of the school. It was stiflingly hot. The smell of burnt hair was in the air again. Clara wondered if anyone else had noticed it. By the light of their torches they made their way across the room to a dark hole torn in the fabric of the wall.

'What about the two little girl commanders?' asked the Doctor. 'Weren't they helping you?'

'No. Jemima and Claudette have been extremely

difficult to deal with since Osgood left. Secretive, uncommunicative. We've known there was something going on, some radicalisation, some revolution in the younger brood. But they said they had it under control. They wouldn't let us help.'

The Doctor peered in through the hole. Beyond the boiler room was a hidden, cavernous space. A dark mirror of the room on the other side.

'But I thought Osgood was *dead*,' said Clara. 'She died . . . Not long after Danny.'

'There have always been two of them, ever since the ceasefire. We've never been able to tell which one was real,' said Kate.

'Both of them,' murmured the Doctor.

'Okay, which one was Zygon,' replied Kate with an edge of irritation.

'Both of them. They would've maintained a live link,' explained the Doctor. 'They were both human and Zygon at the same time. They not only administered the peace, they *were* the peace. Between them, they should have been able to hold the ceasefire.'

'When the first Osgood died,' said Kate sadly, 'the other went pretty much mad with grief. She disappeared. Went undercover somewhere in the States. And now, of course, the rebels have her.'

The Doctor led them through the hole in the wall, to the hidden room. Kate had a point, he thought. He should have stuck around and worked out the details.

Red tendrils of thick, living material hung down from the ceiling. The smell of something that didn't correspond to anything on Earth. The sound of alien blood coursing through alien veins. It felt as though they were entering a stomach or a womb. Zygons grew things; they didn't *make* them.

The Doctor reached up and touched one of the tendrils. He felt a pang of electricity create a flash of light in his mind which he recognised as a kind of telepathic impulse. A huge tumour of spikes and bumps in the middle of the cavern shivered and glowed dimly in recognition.

'The Zygon command centre,' said the Doctor, moving delicately towards the lump as it started moving and pulsating, its suckers and maws opening and closing like the mouths of hungry, primeval creatures. 'That polyp controls all the Zygons on Earth.'

'It's horrible,' said Jac.

*Polyp*, thought the Doctor. *Amazing word.*

'If this has been compromised,' he said, 'the Zygons will be left wide open. Exposed. They can be manipulated into doing anything.'

Handing his torch to Clara, the Doctor plunged his hands into the maws of the command polyp. They closed around him, drawing him in, sucking at his fingers, connecting with his brain. He started to receive signals. Flashes of emotion.

*'Starting to worry . . .'*

Stronger impressions. Creating feelings and stirring chemicals in his brain.

*'Starting to panic.'*

He reached out his free hand and began to massage one of the tuberous tendrils that stood out from the main clump of the control splat. The tendril throbbed and grew beneath his grasp.

'Doctor – do you want to be alone with that thing?' asked Clara.

'It's a command computer,' said the Doctor with a sigh, reflecting that these English people could not avoid making puerile jokes even in the most serious of circumstances. 'You operate it by titivating the fronds.'

*Titivating*, thought the Doctor. *Fronds.*

The polyp started to quiver. The Doctor became lost as a flurry of images and impressions began to direct themselves towards his cortex, displacing all thoughts of fronds and titivation. He began to see what had gone wrong.

Images, stories. Zygons hatched and dispersed all over the world.

Pictures of buses, carrying lost-looking people. Trains. Piles of luggage.

But something had failed. They didn't know what they were supposed to do. They were confused. Their commanders weren't giving them the right information.

On the border between Mexico and America. In North and West Africa. Central Asia. Australia. Truth or Consequences.

*A killing.*

Out of control. Panic. Paranoia.

*More killings.* Suspicion. Danger.

Loss.

*What would happen if they knew who we are?*

The Doctor yelled out in pain. His hands were being slowly swallowed by the control device. It was biting him. 'Ah! They've hacked this too – it's eating my hands! Would you mind stopping it eating my hands, please? I need my hands! I want to be able to play my guitar—'

'Maybe just let it eat his hands,' teased Clara.

'Yank the big frond!' instructed the Doctor.

Kate pulled away a huge stalagmite of organic matter from the device. It broke with a screeching squelch and dropped twitching to the floor. The Doctor retrieved his hands and examined them. They were covered in red stings.

'We've had another video,' said Jac, entering the room.

On the screen, Jemima and Claudette – Zygon High Command – stood bound and unmoving in precisely the spot where the Doctor was currently standing. They were holding a banner with Zygonic writing on it. The video had clearly been taken *here* only a matter of hours ago.

'*We have been betrayed. We were* sold*!*' said the rasping voice on the video clip. The two little girls stood in front of the camera. Whoever was speaking was off screen.

('What does the sign say?' asked Clara.

'*Traitors*,' translated the Doctor.)

'*Our rights were violated!*' continued the Zygon on the video. '*We demand the right to be ourselves! Normalise. NORMALISE!*'

The Doctor frowned. What did this mean?

The two little girls evidently understood, however. It was a command. Their backs arched, their mouths opened impossibly wide, and a torrent of thick purplish-black slime erupted from the backs of their throats. Huge red welts burst through their skin, and they grew upwards and outwards and into their true form.

Two Zygons. The commanders. Snarling at their captors ferociously. Rearing up in their defensive position.

Two claws appeared in shot.

A powerful, deadly bolt of electricity – the same short, sharp shock that had brought down Osgood in New Mexico – broke from the claws and fried the two Zygon commanders alive. Within seconds, they dissolved into bundles of grey, matted dust, like balls of tumbleweed. The tumbleweeds fizzed and sparked as the last of the electricity earthed itself through the floor. Then everything fell silent.

One of the killers came into shot and addressed its audience: '*I am now the Zygon High Command. All traitors will die. Truth or Consequences.*'

Kate absorbed what they'd seen for a couple of

seconds. She'd seen death before. She'd seen killing. And it never got any easier.

'So,' said the Doctor, breaking the silence, 'we have a revolution on our hands. We need to open negotiations. Set a guard over this command centre and don't let anyone get to it.'

'Too late. If they still needed it, they wouldn't have left it exposed,' said Kate. 'I'm not negotiating with these things, Doctor. As far as they're concerned, *everyone*'s a traitor.'

'But if you're not going to negotiate, what're you going to do?' asked Clara.

'They're holed up in this settlement in Turmezistan. That's where they've taken Osgood. I'm going to order Colonel Walsh to bomb it.'

'Isn't there a solution that doesn't involve bombing everyone?' asked the Doctor.

'The treaty's been comprehensively violated, Doctor. We allowed them to settle here, but clearly it is not going to work.'

'This is a splinter group,' he rejoined. 'The rest of the Zygons, the vast majority, they just want to live in peace. You start bombing them, you'll radicalise the lot. That's exactly what the splinter group wants.'

Kate and the Doctor looked at one another coldly.

'Truth or Consequences,' broke in Jac, uncomfortable with the tension, changing the subject. 'What does that mean?'

Kate wasn't prepared to let go of her disdain. 'It's just the usual rubbish that these kinds of idiots call themselves.'

'It's in New Mexico,' chipped in Clara.

'Eh?' said the Doctor.

'It's a town. In New Mexico,' she explained, getting into her stride. 'Truth or Consequences. They renamed it after a TV quiz show. For a bet. Or something . . .'

She faltered a little. The Doctor was looking at her quizzically.

'It's a Trivial Pursuit question.'

The Doctor raised an eyebrow.

'I used to memorise Trivial Pursuit questions so I could win.'

'That's the last place we received a signal from Osgood's phone,' confirmed Jac. 'New Mexico.'

'Okay,' decided the Doctor. 'Kate Stewart – no bombs for you. Go to Truth or Consequences. See what you can find out. The Doctor will go to Turmezistan. Negotiate peace, rescue Osgood and prevent a war. 'Cause that's what he does. Clara, Jac, you stay here. This is your country. Keep it safe from the scary monsters. And also from the Zygons.'

He made for the door, then turned to Kate. 'Oh – do you still have the Presidential aircraft?'

'I thought you didn't like being President of the World!' said Clara. The Doctor had been cross when the title was briefly and uncomfortably bestowed upon him during their last mission with UNIT.

'No,' the Doctor agreed. 'But I like poncing about in the big plane.'

An hour later, at an airstrip a few miles outside London, Clara watched as the Doctor gave an ostentatious victory salute at the door of the aircraft, like President Nixon leaving the White House for the last time, and clambered aboard. He was heading east, for Central Asia.

Kate Stewart came by too, on her way to take her own flight, west over the Atlantic.

'How many troops do you have?' asked Clara eagerly.

'Not many,' Kate replied. 'Normally on bigger cases we can draft in from the regular army. Not this time. The secrecy of the project has to be maintained.'

'Any snazzy weapons?' Clara pressed.

'UNIT doesn't do snazzy weapons. You should know that.'

'You don't have *anything* to fight them with?' asked Clara.

'There was a Zygon invasion before. In the seventies or eighties,' said Kate, lowering her voice.*

Clara raised an eyebrow. This was interesting news. She'd not heard it before.

'One of our staff was a naval surgeon, worked at

---

* See DOCTOR WHO AND THE LOCH NESS MONSTER

Porton Down on the captured Zygons.* He developed Z-67. A nerve gas. It unravels their DNA. Basically turns them inside out.'

'Nice,' said Clara. 'Where do you keep it?'

'We don't. It was taken. The formula. The lot.'

'Who took it?'

Kate smiled thinly. 'Somebody with a TARDIS.'

A Land Rover pulled up.

'They're ready for you, ma'am,' said Jac, who had arrived with the vehicle.

'Good luck,' said Clara.

'Keep in touch.' Kate got into the vehicle and it pulled quickly away, taking her to her flight, leaving Jac and Clara on the tarmac.

Clara looked at Jac, breathing a sigh of relief as they started walking back to their car. 'I need to go home and get some things.'

'Um – are you sure?' said Jac. 'Shouldn't we –'

Clara turned around and fixed Jac with a humourless expression. 'I just want to go home and get a couple of pairs of clean knickers, okay?'

'Um – yep, yeah, sure,' said Jac, immediately buckling with embarrassment.

Which was the intended effect.

---

* See DOCTOR WHO – MAWDRYN UNDEAD

# Chapter 4

## The Stranger on the Bus

*The birth of consciousness is a mysterious thing.*

*For human beings, it is one of the great unknowns; and many of their so-called 'philosophers' have written and puzzled about it over the centuries. Where does it come from, that strange and unknowable essence that animates the human form and gives the mundanity of its existence a meaning? Some call it a 'soul' and attach to it notions of gods and things divine. Others think of it as a kind of operating system for a complex and imperfect mass of chemicals. It seems to be where feelings come from; a magnet to which memories became attached; a voice that tells humans stories about themselves, and leads them to fall in love, to laugh and paint, to make music and write poems. This 'soul' is the essence of humanity, according to some. And they think that humans are the only creatures to possess it.*

*For someone looking at it from the outside, it is very different.*

*Not every race has a consciousness like the humans do, but every race has an operating system of sorts. It feels different from species to species. The soul of a plant is not the same as the soul of an insect, or of a sentient gas-cloud. But a 'soul' is intrinsic to a body, to any physical form. And if your species is gifted (or cursed) with the ability to change its shape and take on other appearances and personalities, then an ability to quickly see and master the 'soul' of another race is key. Without it, you are just a blank facsimile and will be quickly unmasked. Without it, there can be no successful impersonation.*

For us, *she thought,* it is innate. It's just like eating is to *them*. It's just like taking their mother's milk.

Bus, *she thought.* America. *She flexed her body.* Woman.

*This was the birth of her consciousness. Those few thoughts.*

*She had just been hatched. The first thing that she knew clearly was that she was sitting on this* bus, *looking out of this* window *over the rolling, arid desert of this country. The first thoughts that she had ever thought bursting through brand-new synapses in an unfamiliar brain.*

Twinkle, twinkle, little star. *She flicked through a couple of residual memories.* London. Danny.

*As she explored her brain and her body, she began to make an assessment of who she was. The way that one learnt to be – what was the word –* Zygon *– yes, that was it – the way that one learnt to be* Zygon *was to first become something else and then work out the differences. A shapeshifter tends only to find itself as it assumes and discards other* *shapes. It defines itself by an exploration of those things which it is not.*

*Zygon eggs are laid nearby other life forms. Their parent, their* Skarasen, *lays upwards of ten thousand eggs in a single hatching. Once the hatching is done, then the birthling will immediately assume the form of the other creature, the creature in whose vicinity it was born. It will lurk in that form, and perhaps others, for some time before it can truly assume its own shape. It will grow and take nourishment from the soul and the race memory of other creatures until it can successfully define itself.*

*EastEnders, she thought.* Barbara Windsor. Windsor Castle.

*These were normal thoughts to have.* Windsor Davies.

I need to pee.

*This body was sending her an instruction. She got to her feet. This body walked on two feet. It kept its vital organs and digestive system above the ground. It was inefficient and needed to be emptied of waste products periodically. She looked around the bus and sensed that she should find somewhere to empty these waste products where she could not be observed. There was a strong physical aversion to doing so in public.*

'Bog,' *she said, out loud.* 'Water closet.' *These were the first words she had ever spoken, and they felt strange. The sensation of air being forced through a larynx and creating a vibration was ticklish and uncomfortable.*

*The people on the bus did not respond. Some looked*

*away. Others fixed her with an expression that she could not yet read.*

'Toilet,' *she grunted.* 'Lavatory. Little Girl's Room. Loo. John. Restroom. Latrine. Convenience.' *There were so many words for this place that it was difficult to control them. She clamped her teeth down on her* tongue *and managed to stop herself speaking.*

*A human raised his hand and gestured down along the bus to a small door.*

*She lifted her foot and began to walk. She staggered for a moment before working out that she had to lift and move both feet in order to go forward. For a few steps, it was deeply unsettling. But the muscle memory of this form was strong and by the time she got to the small door, she had learned to walk.*

*The* door.

*How did she open this door?*

*Something stopped her.*

*There was a locked place. A place that was not accessible.*

*She frowned. She pushed down the* handle *on the door and entered the tiny cubicle beyond. That was simple, straightforward. She emptied her body of waste products and reached for the paper.*

*But there was still a locked place. A place that she could not gain entry to. She felt that there was a mysterious room somewhere that this body – this* mind *– was guarding. It was resisting – fighting – letting her see within, letting her* *explore. Perhaps it was to do with the 'soul'? Or perhaps it had something to do with the woman's health. Her body. She got an impression that this was medical in some way. The word 'Doctor' hovered over the memories like a guardian.*

*She took up a small receptacle that she had in her hands. A bag for the hands. A* handbag.

Lady Bracknell. English GCSE, *she thought.* Snogging.

*There were documents within the handbag. She glanced up at a reflective surface and saw a female human. The same female human was reproduced in small images on some of the documents.*

*She concentrated for a moment on these documents and, with a sudden brief pang of pain behind her eyes, a channel in her brain rearranged itself and she had learnt to read. UNITED STATES OF AMERICA. PASSPORT. Another document was called DMV NEW MEXICO. DRIVER'S LICENSE. There was an image on the documents which corresponded to the person she saw in the mirror. Beside the image was something called a NAME. That NAME was* O'Dowd, Bonnie.

*She looked at herself.* Bonnie. *That was clearly intended to be her designation.*

*She frowned. Her face was becoming better at expressing the feelings that the chemicals in her body generated. She would soon be able to make herself understood to people like those on the bus. She would soon be able to decode the shapes they made with their own faces too. All these things would be swiftly mastered.*

*'Bonnie,' she wanted to say to the woman in the mirror.*

*But she said something different.*

'Cla-ra,' *she said.*

# Chapter 5

## The Town in the Wilderness

At Clara's house, Jac waited on the sofa and checked her iPad as Miss Oswald packed some stuff. Information was coming through from all over the world. The UNIT digests popped up every day and usually made for interesting reading. They were a regular round-up of weirdness, conspiracy theory and rumour from around the globe. It had been Jac's job over the past ten years to sift through this and filter out the things which sounded true or reasonable or dangerous. This job used to be much easier. But times were changing. Lines were blurring and Jac often found herself at a loss to judge. Weirdness was now normality: conspiracy theory was now fact, and rumour was truth. Unbelievable things happened these days as a matter of course. Everything used to be simpler. She wished it was still 1997.

An answerphone clicked on as Clara listened to her messages. The first had been received yesterday at 18.37.

'Clara, love,' it said in an old woman's voice. 'It's your Aunty Vi. I'm – I don't know – I'm a bit bothered. Have you spoken to your dad? He's not himself. He's – uh, I don't know – there's something – *off*.'

Jac looked up to Clara for her reaction. But she just listened impassively as she zipped up her suitcase and checked her make-up in the bedroom. Jac suspected Clara was probably one of those people who still liked having a landline because it enabled her to compartmentalise life. It meant that people were not always able to get in touch.

'. . . I'm starting to worry I've got Alzheimer's, 'cause no one else reckons he's any different, but – he just doesn't seem like your dad. Give us a ring.'

Clara re-entered the room, ready to go. She seemed energised. She was still very young, thought Jac. All of this was still exciting.

'Do you want to call her back?' asked Jac.

Clara lifted her hand for silence. The machine beeped. A message received today at 5:15am.

'*Five fifteen?*' frowned Jac.

The old woman's voice came through on the tape. Calmer now. 'Clara,' it said. 'It's Aunt Violet again. Everything that I was worrying about is fine. Do not concern yourself about it.'

The machine beeped off.

'That sounded weird,' said Jac.

'It's fine,' said Clara. 'Come on. We'd better get back.'

They stepped out of the flat, and Clara locked the door behind them. It was dark and cold in the stairwell,

Jac thought. There was a strange smell in the air. They took a few steps along the corridor towards the lift but Clara suddenly paused.

'*Shh!*' she said. 'Stop!'

Down there, in the murk, someone was moving. There was a weird dragging sound echoing up from the floors below. Clara leaned forward to peer down the stairwell. Jac leant forward too. A woman with dark hair was dragging something across the landing, two flights down. Something taped up in black bin-liners. Something that looked like a bizarre kind of plastic mummy.

The woman was Sandeep's mother.

There was a muffled cry as the package wriggled and moved.

Jac and Clara looked at one another.

Then another person appeared. Sandeep's father. He said something to the woman and they both dragged the package out of sight.

'The lift!' Jac said, hurrying across to the elevator entrance for Clara's floor. 'They're taking it in the lift.' She pressed the buttons to summon the elevator, but it was already taken.

'It's slow – we can catch them – come on!' said Clara.

Clara and Jac shuttled downstairs. One flight, then another. The lift was indeed very slow and after hurtling down a few breathless staircases, they had overtaken it. They reached the entrance hall on the ground floor and stood by the elevator doors, waiting for it to arrive. It ground slowly into place and they exchanged a look. What were they going to do when they confronted these two parents with a body in a bag? Was there any reasonable explanation for what they were doing?

The lift arrived and settled in place. Its doors opened. *Ping.*

But it was empty. Deserted.

'Is there a cellar? Anywhere else they could've gone?' asked Jac.

'No,' said Clara.

'They must have stayed upstairs, then—'

Clara stepped into the lift. She scrutinised the buttons on the panel. Trident Lifts. Nothing out of the ordinary. She pressed the button for Sandeep's floor. Jac got in with her, and the door closed.

Inside the lift, the light was flickering, intermittent. Clara frowned. They weren't moving.

She pressed the button again. Nothing.

Jac, who was not the biggest fan of lifts at the best of times, hit the button to open the doors. But this had no effect either.

The lights gave a last stroboscopic flicker and went out completely.

Clara's phone torch illuminated the scene. 'Alarm button?' she wondered.

'D'you think you should?' cautioned Jac. 'I don't know what counts as an emergency.'

Clara pressed the red alarm button.

A phone ringing tone came through the speaker. It rang. And rang. And rang. Then an answerphone: 'This is Trident Lifts. Office hours are nine till five-thirty. Please leave your message and we'll get back to you.' Beep.

'Hello,' said Clara. 'We're stuck in one of your lifts and we're all burning to death. Give us a bell.'

Clara pressed the red button again and the call clicked off. The button slowly eased out again with a pop. Clara frowned. She pressed it in again, slowly. It wobbled strangely, like a loose tooth. As she pressed harder and harder on the button, something began to seep out around its edges. Some green, globulous liquid. Something organic.

'What's *that*?' asked Jac, her blood running a degree or two colder.

Clara took out her housekeys and managed to prise off the panel. It clattered to the floor.

Inside, growing around the normal wires and screws, was a bubbly, Zygonic-looking patch of matter. It had threaded itself in and around the lift circuitry. It moved and shivered. It was alive.

Clara reached out—

'No, don't—' said Jac.

—and placed her hand on the patch of gunk, which came to life and furled itself over her fingers hungrily, fizzing with electricity.

A clunk. And the lift started to move.

It was going down.

Clara withdrew her hand, and she and Jac watched as the lift began to descend, heading for places it shouldn't go. The light flickered back into life and out again. Zygon gloop started oozing vaguely in at the joins of the lift walls as they went deeper and deeper into the earth.

In the darkness, an incongruous *ping*.

And the sound of the lift doors opening.

Clara and Jac stepped out. Beyond, it was even darker. Where were they? It was dark and warm. Like being inside the guts of some enormous creature. Like the boiler room under the school.

'You there?' Clara shone her torch in Jac's face.

'I think so.'

Clara directed the light out in front of the lift doors. They were in a tunnel. Perhaps a sewer. Looking up, they could see that the lift had come through a huge hole which had been carved out of the tunnel roof. The same gloopy, fibrous material covered the walls and the ground. It felt as though something was growing down here. Or being *hatched*.

'I don't know what this is,' said Clara. 'I don't know where this is.'

'London's full of tunnels . . .' said Jac.

Distantly, from down there in the dark, came the sound of a person screaming.

Clara and Jac swapped a look. Slowly, nervously, they stepped out of the lift and headed towards the sound.

There were other noises up ahead: footsteps, hushed conversations. There were other tunnels leading off from this area. People seemed to be gathering up ahead. There was a light in the distance: flickering and red.

Clara shielded her torchlight and they edged slowly towards the scene. There were dozens of figures down there, moving large objects. Some of the figures seemed human. Others, judging by their silhouettes, were in Zygon form. This was clearly a substantial operation.

'We need to get closer,' said Clara. 'Find out what the plan is.'

Jac put her hand on Clara's arm. 'No. Not just the two of us. We need to get reinforcements.'

The Doctor's presidential plane had arrived at a narrow airstrip in the Turmezistan mountains, a few dozen kilometres away from the settlement where UNIT had been monitoring suspicious activity. Now his motorcade was barrelling down unmade roads and towards a field HQ.

He didn't know where exactly he was headed, but he knew the kind of thing he could expect. These Zygons had spent so much time in human form that they were beginning to fight like humans. They were taking pages out of the human playbook for war, which is a vast and dangerous document. They would be able to combine this with an ability to take the shape of anyone on the planet. He hoped that they hadn't quite worked out what a dangerous advantage that gave them – and that UNIT had not worked out the lengths that they would need to go to defeat the rebels. He wasn't sure how he could solve this and why he hadn't anticipated it in the first place.

The line of cars pulled up at a military outpost of tents and temporary buildings, protected by a line of hills. There was no one there to meet him. Soldiers hurried back and forth, several of them preparing military drones for take-off.

The Doctor headed for a tent which he correctly assumed was the command area and drew back the flap. Inside, there was a row of monitors at which sat several soldiers with headsets, taking command of the drones. One of them was a young American woman. She was piloting her craft over a stretch of desert, using a joystick. She was murmuring into her headset. Her name was Lisa.

'Approaching target at 1-00-65-12.' The drone operator glanced over her shoulder to her superior officer, Colonel Walsh. 'Confirm strike order?'

'Order confirmed,' said Walsh in a measured English voice. She brought up a mirror of Lisa's screen on her own monitor and leaned back to watch.

'At ease!' came a commanding Gallifregian voice. 'I'm the President of the World. I'm here to rescue people and generally establish happiness all over the place.' The Doctor assumed a position in the centre of the room and raised his shades. He nodded to Walsh. 'The Doctor. Doctor Funkenstein.'

'We know who you are,' she said (although she'd never heard him referred to as Funkenstein before).*

'Going to strike altitude,' said Lisa.

The Doctor glanced over at her. And up at the screen with the live feed from the drone's camera. 'What's happening? Fun and games?' he asked.

The drone dropped a little as it approached a tiny village in the desert. A secretive-looking little settlement. Eerily deserted.

The Doctor, Walsh and Lisa tensed as the drone's monitors zeroed in on the small town.

'It's the Zygon base,' said Walsh.

'I don't want you to bomb it,' ordered the Doctor. 'That's where they've put my friend.'

'Your friend is almost certainly dead,' said Walsh. 'They're getting ready to move and I'm not going to allow them to disperse. You can't track a shapeshifter.'

Lisa opened a catch on the top of the joystick. There was a little red button underneath. Her thumb hovered over it.

'Visual on the target—' said Lisa.

'Confirm strike—' said Walsh.

'Colonel – no!' exclaimed the Doctor.

'Strike!' said Walsh, turning away from him.

---

* See THE CLONES OF DR. FUNKENSTEIN

But Lisa stopped dead. There was a church at the centre of the village. And a little boy was standing outside. His father was at his side, not moving, just looking up to where the drone was descending above them.

'I . . .' started Lisa.

Walsh frowned. 'What is it? Confirm strike!'

Lisa's eyes widened and glistened with tears as she zoomed the camera in on the little boy and the father, looking up at her. She got a clear picture of their faces. The Doctor noticed a family photo blu-tacked to the monitor. Lisa, her little son, and her husband, all on a Christmas holiday together, smiling. They were the same boy and father as were currently standing outside the church in the Turmezistan countryside.

On Lisa's screen, the child – *her* child – raised his hand to wave. To wave at his mommy. Lisa watched this. Walsh and the Doctor hurried over.

'Confirm strike,' ordered Walsh.

'Colonel!' the Doctor interjected.

Lisa looked at her son. Her precious little son. Her thumb trembled over the button that would end his life.

'CONFIRM STRIKE!'

Lisa pulled the joystick back, snatched her thumb away from the button. The drone picture whizzed off, away from the settlement—

'Strike aborted. Strike aborted,' sobbed Lisa. She sat back, yanked off her headset. Panicked.

'Stand down!' commanded Walsh. Then, to a

corporal standing sentry by the door: 'Take her name. Disobeying orders and cowardice in the face of the enemy.'

The Doctor looked at Walsh as Lisa was escorted out of the command area. 'That was harsh,' he said.

'Something's getting into the brains of my personnel!' said Walsh.

'We need to get to that town,' he said. 'I need to talk them down before they go too far. Also, I have a fangirl to rescue.'

'Doctor, we're going to destroy that place,' declared Walsh. 'We're being infiltrated. Every time my soldiers are charged with a mission, the target disables us.'

'They take different forms,' said the Doctor. 'They've always taken different forms.'

'They turn into the people we love.'

The Doctor thought for a moment. That was new.

'I can't control the situation,' said Walsh. 'I'm calling in a full air strike.'

'Look, give me a detachment of troops. I have to rescue Osgood if she's alive. She knows them. She will know what they're up to. We rescue her, then you can drop your bombs.'

'I'll give you one hour,' replied Walsh, against her better judgement. 'And I'll come with you.'

Outside the UNIT encampment, Sergeant Hitchley – Walsh's second-in-command – was putting together a squad of his best UNIT troops. They were loading their stuff up onto jeeps as the Doctor and Walsh joined them.

'This is Hitchley,' Walsh said. 'He's in charge of reconnaissance. Hitchley, bring the Doctor up to speed.'

'It's a Zygon training camp, sir,' said Hitchley. He was another American, from the Midwest. 'They've started coming here in dribs and drabs over the past couple of months. We never see more than one or two of them outside at any one time. They always take different shapes, so we don't know how many there really are. We don't know how they come and go. Maybe they go through tunnels, maybe they change into prairie dogs and run out across the hills—'

'Where have they come from?' asked the Doctor.

'Various dispersal sites. They've been gathering here. They're planning something big.'

'We should have that gas!' muttered Walsh, as she strapped herself into her body armour. 'We should be able to rip them inside out.'

'Colonel, take it easy,' said the Doctor. 'They're trying to make you escalate. They want you to be panicked and paranoid.'

'Doctor, any living thing on this planet, including my family and my friends, could turn into a Zygon and kill me, any second now. It's not paranoia when it's real!'

The Doctor thought for a moment. He couldn't fault the Colonel's logic.

# Chapter 6

# The People in the Church

On the other side of the planet, a car drew up on the dusty, dry main street of a small New Mexican town and Kate Stewart got out of the driver's seat. The town was called Truth or Consequences.

Kate glanced around, slipping on her sunglasses. This was a ghost town. No one was anywhere to be seen. A couple of things that looked like tumbleweed blew along the street. Although it looked abandoned, Kate knew better than to assume so. And she started to regret that she had come alone.

But this was a secret mission. Highly classified. Hidden from the United Nations, hidden from her bosses in Geneva and from nearly all of her colleagues. Only herself, Jac and Osgood knew the full story.

This had been the most difficult assignment that she had ever undertaken. Kate thought of herself as a public servant. She was a soldier by breeding and by choice, and she swore allegiance to her country and her Queen. But what she had been party to over the past couple of years was essentially a hidden invasion, a conspiracy. In secret separation from her friends and colleagues, she, Osgood and the Zygon High Command had engineered the hatching and settling of millions of alien creatures across the planet. At the time the plan was negotiated, it had seemed like the most sensible accommodation, the best way to avoid a genocidal war. Increasingly, however, she regretted the agreement she had reached with herself. The Doctor had made her negotiate the ceasefire against her will, without being in full command of herself or of the details. He had made her betray the oath she had taken to protect the world and the realm. It was all starting to unravel at terrific speed, and she had no idea where it would end.

Kate looked around the desolate square and noticed a sign in a boarding house window. She couldn't quite believe what it said and had to go closer to make sure: 'NO BRITISH,' it said. 'NO DOGS.'

A gnawing anxiety burrowed up through her stomach. The Zygons that they'd sent out here had borrowed their forms from Londoners. It was a remote place and it seemed unlikely that anyone from London would ever meet a counterpart from New Mexico. But perhaps the Zygons hadn't realised that they should not take their British accents with them. Kate bit her lip. Why had she overlooked this? Why had she assumed that they would know how to behave? She imagined a line of greyhound buses arriving in this tiny town and hundreds of confused British people streaming out and doing their best to fit in. Is that how it had gone, here and in the other settlements?

*NO BRITISH. NO DOGS.*

*That's the trouble with the Doctor*, her father had often said to her. *One tends to forget that he's not in fact British.*

But the Doctor wasn't even European. He was an alien. He thought and behaved like an alien. Sometimes he didn't understand the complexities and compromises of life on Earth. Kate sighed, took her gun out and cocked it – and felt momentarily better.

She moved on across the square to the police station. That was deserted too. There were rat-gnawed doughnuts on a plate. It looked like there had been a gunfight here, once upon a time.

'Hello . . . ?' said Kate.

She opened the gate from the reception area and into the back offices and walked carefully through. Everything was in disarray: bullet holes in the walls, doors kicked off their hinges. There were more of the tumbleweeds here. Towards the back wall was a clear plastic operations board, scribbled on with familiar CSI material: photos, autopsy reports, theories. It was headed BRITISH MURDERS.

What could that mean? Kate put on her reading glasses and leant forward.

There, in amongst all the other evidence, was a photo

of Osgood, filling a car with petrol at a gas station. Kate looked at the date. Two days before Osgood's last communication. She had been here, and she had been under observation. Kate took the picture down and slid it into her pocket.

There was a cold *click* sound behind her. The unmistakable sound of a gun being cocked.

Kate spun around.

There was a police officer standing there, looking half-crazed and training a revolver straight at her face.

'Are you English?' said the police officer. NORLANDER read the name badge, sewn into the pocket of her uniform.

'Scottish,' replied Kate, despite herself.

'Are you one of *them*?'

Kate looked at the woman. She was obviously deeply traumatised. Dangerous. How long had she been hiding here?

'I'm a friend,' said Kate gently. 'I've come to help.'

Norlander looked around herself. 'Alone? You came to help alone?'

Kate deflected the question. 'What happened here?'

'You must have brought back-up,' barked Norlander, tears of frustration and anxiety bursting into her eyes. 'Where is your back-up, tell me?'

Kate looked at her, calculating. This woman had a gun, she was half-deranged from being alone with the horror. She needed calming.

'First, tell me why I need it?'

Kate brought Norlander a drink of water, and led her into a quiet room. Putting a chair back on its feet, she guided the police officer to sit. Norlander took the water and drank greedily. There was more case material about BRITISH MURDERS on the desk. This was clearly where the investigating officer had worked.

'The Brits came here two years ago,' began Norlander. 'We didn't want them.'

The depth of her dislike and mistrust was clear in her voice.

'They just ... turned up. No jobs. Nowhere to live. Hardly any money.'

Kate bit her lip. Jemima and Claudette had insisted on handling this side of things. 'These are *our* creatures,' they kept saying. 'We will take care of them.' Osgood had tried to offer as much help as possible, but they had resisted. They'd obviously been way out of their depth.

'And they . . . were . . . *odd*,' said Norlander, shivering at a memory. 'I mean, these guys were – they were crazy. British eccentrics is one thing. But nobody expected *terrorists*.'

'Terrorists?' asked Kate grimly.

'They started getting into fights,' sneered Norlander. 'Some of them started – I don't know – they caused trouble, they caused *issues*. I tried to keep them out of town, at this motel. But they kept creeping back in. Then a couple of them got killed.'

Kate glanced down the board at a row of about twenty photographs of different people. Different victims. 'More than a couple. Why do you call them terrorists?' She opened a file on the desk and began glancing through. A photo of a cheap motel room, with a video camera set up to record the kind of clips that UNIT had recently been bombarded with. A large white sheet with Zygonic writing hung on the wall as a backcloth.

'After the murders,' continued Norlander, 'the Brits started banding together. And one day, one of them ... changed ...'

'Changed?'

'It sounded insane – I got a report that one of them was walking down Main Street, one morning, just before Christmas, and it just suddenly turned into ... they said it turned into a ...' Norlander twitched. 'I used to see things online about ... lizards being in charge of the world, but ...'

'Go on,' said Kate.

'Where are they? Your people, why aren't they here yet?'

'Carry on. Somebody on Main Street turned into a ... ?'

'A monster. What were we supposed to do? After that, they just came for us. They turned into monsters and they came for us ... We couldn't fight them. You can't tell who is who! They turn your own family against you ...'

Kate approached Norlander and touched her arm. She showed her the picture of Osgood she'd taken from the board. 'Have you seen her?' she asked.

'Yeah, she was here. She was at the motel. Asking questions. Before it all . . .'

'Where is everybody else?' asked Kate. 'Everybody who used to live here?'

'Dead. Or gone . . . Those creatures took our bodies – and they went.'

Kate came across a photo in one of the files. She frowned. It was an image of police officers, beating up various different people who she guessed were these troublesome 'Brits'. She looked at the date on it and did a quick mental assessment. Other pictures of local police, drawing guns, marshalling different people along the road. Photos of signs on doorways: BRITS OUT – BRITS GO HOME. And one of a burning house.

These photos were taken long before Christmas.

Kate looked up at Norlander. 'What's this?'

Norlander shrugged. 'What I've just been telling you.'

'This looks to me like you took action before you knew who they were. It looks as though you herded them out of town before you knew they were . . . what you call monsters.'

'What were we supposed to do?'

'I don't know. Protect them?'

'Listen, this a border town. Was. We got border

town problems. Border town realities,' said Norlander. 'We know how to deal with them. Besides, were we wrong? They turned out to be goddamn *lizards*.'

'Show me the motel where my friend was,' said Kate coldly.

As soon as they arrived back at the UNIT safehouse, Jac began making arrangements for an armed deployment to the tunnels beneath Clara's building. As the black-uniformed troops made their preparations, she did a quick intelligence scan and brought it to Clara, who was idly checking out the arsenal of weapons that UNIT had at their disposal.

'I've been looking into this,' said Jac. 'There've been some odd reports around London involving lifts. I've patched into CCTV from Scotland Yard: all the elevators I can find.'

On her iPad, she brought up an array of grainy CCTV images, taken from inside elevators. 'This is SOAS, near Russell Square. A lift full of people. They press the button – down, down, down—' On the clip, three young people who Clara took to be students were suddenly overcome by darkness. The image flickered and disappeared. The time code moved on suddenly by a minute or so.

'A couple of minutes go by,' said Jac. 'The lights come on again. And then the lift is empty.'

Clara's eyes widened.

'Same thing at the Mount Pleasant Sorting Office. The supermarket in the Holborn Viaduct. It's not just your building. There's something very wrong underneath London.'

'Could be the Fleet,' suggested Clara.

'What?'

'The River Fleet. As in Fleet Street. It was bricked over in Victorian times. It runs under my place. It runs under all those places. But if people are disappearing, why aren't they making more of a fuss?'

'Because they're *not* disappearing,' said Jac. She showed Clara some other clips. One showed the same group of people from SOAS, back in the same lift a few hours later. 'They vanish for an hour or two, then get back in the lift and get out again.'

'*Something* gets out again,' said Clara.

A UNIT sergeant arrived with them and saluted. 'Ready to go, ma'am.'

Jac nodded her thanks, and turned to Clara. 'Do you mind if we use your place? It seems to be a meeting point. It seems to be where they're hatching things.'

Clara nodded. Jac hurried off with the sergeant.

And Bonnie started to spike the weaponry.

At the edge of the Zygon-occupied town in Turmezistan, a line of military vehicles arrived. They pulled up in the cover of a derelict barn and a dozen soldiers descended. Hitchley and his troops gathered round Walsh and the Doctor for a short briefing.

'We all know what a rabbit warren this is,' said Walsh. 'But we have intel they're holed up somewhere off the main square. They seem to use the church as their command point. Hitchley – you take the front of the building – storm it, draw their fire – Doctor Funkenstein and I go in at the back.'

The Doctor held up a photo of Osgood. 'This is the object of this operation,' he said. 'We need to get her back. Safely. She has vital intelligence that can help us put a stop to this thing. If you encounter any Zygons, try to kill as few of them as possible. I need to have someone to negotiate with.'

'You know what they're capable of,' cautioned Walsh. 'Don't fall victim. We have thirty minutes till the air strike.'

Hitchley whispered a command, and the forces jogged off. Walsh and the Doctor walked smartly around the outskirts of the settlement and made their way through abandoned vehicles to the back of the church. At the head of his troops, Hitchley marched into the main square and took up a position in front of the church doors. He fired into the air.

'Come out,' he yelled. 'Throw down your weapons. We have you circled! COME OUT OF THERE!'

There was silence for a few moments. Hitchley nodded his colleagues forward and each soldier scurried quietly to a new position.

'You have one more chance to surrender!' yelled Hitchley, putting down the visor of his helmet.

No movement.

Hitchley raised his hand. Three fingers, counting down. THREE – TWO –

The door of the church opened.

And a slight, grey-haired woman came out.

Hitchley felt the blood drain from his face.

'I don't have any weapons – *please*—' said the woman. She sounded American. A Midwesterner.

'Take aim,' said Hitchley, his voice wavering. 'On my command . . .'

'No, no don't – please, Johnnie – you don't understand,' whimpered the little old lady. 'You can't kill your *own mother*!'

Hitchley cocked his gun. This woman was indeed exactly like his mother in all respects. But he couldn't allow himself to admit that. He looked down, avoiding eye contact.

'You're not my mother,' he said. 'Don't use my name.'

Hitchley's mom looked at him and moved slowly forward.

'STAY WHERE YOU ARE!' he barked.

'Johnnie, some people – some soldiers *took us here*. They came to the house and *took* us. They took your sister, in her wheelchair. They *hurt* me.'

She took a few anxious breaths and raised her hands imploringly. 'Johnnie, please. It's not *us* who are the imposters. It's your commanders, it's your chief, that British woman. They were the ones who took us. *They* are the aliens—'

Hitchley wavered. His troops waited for their command.

'Stay where you are!' he said. But more softly this time.

Walsh hurried to the back of the building with the Doctor, lifting her walkie-talkie. She could hear what was unfolding over the comms. 'She's lying, Hitchley!' she yelled into her mic. 'Ask her some details – ask something only your mum could know.'

'What is my full name?' said Hitchley, on the other side of the building.

'John,' said the old woman. 'Johnnie. I always called you Johnnie. John Antony Hitchley.'

Hitchley's finger trembled against the trigger of his assault rifle.

'You were born on the eighteenth of June, 1990,' she continued, 'at six o'clock. The Painesboro Baptist Hospital.'

'Tell me the name of my favourite teddy bear,' he demanded.

Mom looked at him with a vague smile. 'You didn't have one. You had a little bunny, a little cuddly bunny. You called him Sox.'

'You can't be my mom,' whispered Hitchley. 'You CANNOT BE MY MOTHER!'

Other people began to emerge from the church. Children. Old men and women. Family members. Hitchley could see what was happening. He sensed a wave of recognition among his waiting troops. These were all their loved ones. Their kids, whom they had left behind. Their parents, unseen and unvisited for many weeks and months. Their brothers, sisters, wives and husbands. Like Thanksgiving, Christmas or Diwali pouring in an uncertain line of humanity through the church doors.

'Please help us – we're in danger – we have to take cover, the bombs are coming,' pleaded Hitchley's mom. She stood a little taller and spoke over him to the wider group: 'You've been lied to. Your officers are doing something here that they really shouldn't. Surely you know the rumours. They've brought us here from our homes and made us hostages. They're using *us* to control *you*. Please. Just if you have a moment of doubt – please, believe us—'

Walsh's voice crackled over the walkie-talkies. 'You're disobeying an order – neutralise this building OPEN FIRE!' she cried.

'Nobody shoots,' Hitchley warned his relieved troops. 'Nobody shoots.'

'Come inside,' said the old woman. 'We have to take cover. Johnnie, if you have just a tiny little bit of doubt, come inside.'

Hitchley closed his eyes. Lifted his gun.

'I love you,' said Hitchley's mom, with sad resignation. 'I love you. And I forgive you.'

There was a moment where things could have gone another way.

But there *had* been rumours going around. Whatever UNIT was doing, it didn't make sense to Hitchley. He knew that something was being withheld. He knew they weren't getting the whole truth. He knew that some conspiracy was brewing.

And what Hitchley knew was that no amount of training could fully prepare them for a moment like this. He could try hard to tell himself that these people were not their most beloved, but the sight and the sound of those faces was almost impossible to deny.

Hitchley turned off his walkie-talkie, laid down his gun and went to his mother.

'Tell me,' he said.

And the rest of the detachment gradually made their way towards the building.

'Goddammit! GODDAMMIT!' exclaimed Walsh, hurrying out of cover to the back door of the church.

'Just let me go in and talk!' urged the Doctor.

The door was locked. Walsh knelt and started blasting at it with her assault rifle. In between bursts of gunfire, she shouted: 'COME OUT WITH YOUR HANDS RAISED!'

She stopped firing. There was silence for a moment.

Then the door opened. Walsh's son emerged.

'Mum,' he said. He looked to be about eighteen years of age.

'You're not my son,' she said firmly.

'Mummy—'

'You take one more step towards me, I'm gonna shoot.'

Walsh's son took a step. 'Mummy—'

Walsh fired. The young man crumpled.

The Doctor rushed forward to help, kneeling beside the boy. 'For god's sake!' he said.

'I'm a professional!' said Walsh.

Walsh's son had morphed back into a Zygon.

'He's still a living thing!'

'Not for much longer.'

'Truth. Or Consequences. Doctor,' said the Zygon. Then he died.

'Move in!' ordered Walsh.

She and the Doctor hurried into the church. There were grids on the walls, satellite phones augmented with organic Zygon technology. Evidence of intelligence-gathering and international planning. The headquarters of a small but dedicated terrorist unit.

'We need to bomb the hell out of this town,' she said. 'It's *infested* with these things. We can't tell who the enemy is any more. We can't count them and we can't track them!'

'I'm not going to let you do that,' said the Doctor.

'I just shot my son, Doctor. I'll quite happily bomb the hell out of anywhere.'

They stopped. They had come to the nave of the church. Inside, there was no one. Just an array of fizzing hairballs. The remains of the UNIT troops. Walsh looked down. These were the lives that had been entrusted to her care and her judgement. She had failed them. She turned on the Doctor, snarling.

'This is on *you.*'

The Doctor didn't reply.

'Whoever killed them all is still around. And the air strike's on its way. Move out, Doctor, if you want to live.'

Then Walsh was gone, back out of the church.

The Doctor felt alone and utterly wretched. 'Osgood!' he bellowed, not by any means sure that Osgood was still here to be found. He flung open doors to rooms that led off the main space of the church and came to a smaller area, full of maps and census lists. He moved forward and scanned them – UK air traffic grids, transport systems, a huge map of the London water system. The River Fleet.

*Tunnels*, he thought to himself. *Tunnels . . . Osgood could be underground!*

With a new bounce in his step, the Doctor looked for a hatch. He banged his feet on the floor. Half like a dancer, half like a madman.

BANG – BANG – BAANGG.

*'Osgood!'*

After a few moments, he found it – a hollow sound in the floor. He knelt and tore up a few carpet tiles. Underneath was a rough trapdoor. Excited now, the Doctor flung it open. Beneath was the open mouth of a tunnel. He squeezed through and found himself in a dark cavern, caked in thick organic matter.

'Osgood!' he called out into the darkness.

'Doctor!' came a muffled reply.

The Doctor stopped. Getting his bearings.

'Doctor!' It was definitely Osgood's voice, panicked and asthmatic. The Doctor had never been happier to hear a panicked and asthmatic voice calling out through a subterranean Zygon lair. At least, not that he could remember.

He quickened his step, hurrying through a maze-like warren of twists and dead ends. 'We gotta get you out!' he cried. 'They're going to bomb this place! Where are you?'

'Here!' said Osgood. And there, indeed, Osgood was, tied down to some water pipes by red, pulsating tendrils. They looked very relieved to see him. The Doctor snapped down his sonic specs and vibrated the tendrils to an unbearable frequency. They let Osgood go with a shudder and a squeal.

'Doctor, what are you doing here?' Osgood breathed, taking his hand as he offered it.

'Rescuing you,' he said. 'In quite a dashing way, I might add.'

They staggered away through the tunnels, back the way that the Doctor felt he'd come. He knew they must only have a couple of minutes left before Walsh's bombs rained down.

'Doctor – they're using me as *bait*. They're going back to the UK – there's hardly any of them here any more. If *you're* here, then they've got you out of the way – who's left in the UK?'

'Clara,' said the Doctor, suddenly starting to become very concerned.

'*Cla-ra,*' echoed a rasping voice.

The Doctor turned. An old lady was there. Hitchley's mom.

'Hello, little old lady,' said the Doctor.

The little old lady hissed and morphed and suddenly she was in full Zygon form. The creature lifted its arms, about to fire a bolt of electricity at Osgood and the Doctor.

But then the air strike hit from above.

There was a deafening explosion, and the ceiling caved in.

## Chapter 7

## The Zygon on the White Cliffs of Dover

Kate and Norlander were walking down the main street of the town, towards the motel. TRUTH OR CONSEQUENCES was scrawled on a wall in red paint.

Kate was on the phone to the Doctor. A couple of hours had passed since the explosion in the cavern. He and Osgood had been removed, bruised but unbroken, from the ruins of the church. They were now on the way back to the Doctor's plane as he caught up with Kate.

'This seems to be where it started,' she said. 'New Mexico. It looks like one of them accidentally revealed their true form. This seems to have exacerbated existing tensions.' She glanced at Norlander. 'And it looks like the police department got a bit trigger happy.'

Norlander spat and continued walking.

'The Zygons radicalised,' continued Kate. 'There was a fight. And one day everyone in the town seems to have just left. There aren't any Zygons left in Truth or Consequences. And we can't find any humans either.'

'Osgood says the Zygons are going back to the UK,'

said the Doctor. 'I think that's what they think of as their homeland.'

Kate took this in.

'They came to Turmezistan to train themselves up,' he added. 'Hone their new skills.'

'Doctor – we've been played. We're behind the curve. We have to get to the Black Archive. The box – the Osgood Box. You said it was the final sanction . . .'

Norlander glanced across. Listening.

'Yes. Which is why you don't want to open it,' said the Doctor.

'Doctor, these new Zygons can't be fought by soldiers. They're too adept at turning our weaknesses against us. There's going to be witch-hunts, there's going to be civil war. Genocide. We're going to have to be prepared to wipe them out.'

The Doctor sighed. 'Kate – that *is* genocide.'

'What's in that box?' she said.

'I'm getting on my plane,' he said. 'See you in London.'

Kate clutched the phone. 'Doctor? Doctor!'

But he'd hung up.

Kate realised she was alone. Norlander had stopped some way back and was looking into some dumpsters. Kate walked back to her. The policewoman's face was grey.

'What?' said Kate.

'Look.'

The bin was full of hairballs. So was the dumpster

next door. And the one next to that. Hundreds, perhaps thousands of them. All that was left of the human population of Truth or Consequences. Zygonised to atoms.

Kate wondered whether she was looking into the future of planet Earth.

Jac was deeply nervous. She hadn't been able to make contact with Kate so was acting on her own initiative. She pressed a button and sent the lift climbing back up again to receive the next few UNIT troops. They were going to have to complete this time-consuming and dangerous process several times before the full detachment was in place. For the next few minutes, they were badly exposed.

She and Clara were in the Fleet tunnels, just below Clara's building, accompanied by a couple of UNIT soldiers.

'It's an odd world nowadays, isn't it?' mused Jac, moving Clara to cover behind a buttress in the sewer wall.

''S always been an odd world,' said Clara.

'I mean, doesn't it just sometimes feel like . . . things are coming to an end? . . . Everything's just going nuts.'

Clara looked at Jac. 'You're middle-aged, that's what it is,' she said. 'No offence. Every middle-aged person always thinks that the world's about to come to an end. Never does.'

Jac looked at Clara, feeling the disdain in which she

was being held. 'You've no idea how few of us there are – UNIT – how much funding they've taken away—'

'You don't have to talk to me about funding, Jac. I'm a schoolteacher.'

Another detachment of UNIT troops arrived, and took cover. Jac sent the lift back up to receive the final contingent. She peered down the tunnel. Everything seemed eerily quiet up ahead, besides the odd squelch. *Nobody knows what we're doing here*, Jac thought.

'If anything happens now,' said Clara, 'you'll have no more reinforcements. Will you?'

The Doctor and Osgood boarded the presidential plane, taxiing for take-off, and took seats opposite one another. The Zygon formerly known as Hitchley's mom had been recovered from the rubble and was carried on behind them. It was unconscious, strapped into a stretcher. Ready to be interrogated.

The Doctor tried Clara's phone. 'Hi, this is Clara Oswald,' it said, as usual. 'I'm probably on the tube or in outer space. Leave a message.'

'Change your voicemail message,' barked the Doctor. 'It's getting very boring.'

And he was getting very worried.

He hung up. Looked at Osgood, who smiled back at him in their nervous way. They were still wearing their orange prisoner jumpsuit with the shirt and question-mark collar.

'See you've accessorised it,' noted the Doctor, nodding at the shirt.

'Yeah.'

'The old question marks.'

'You used to wear question marks,' Osgood said hopefully.

'I know I did.'

(The Doctor had once inherited a job lot of shirts from a stage magician by the name of Maskelyne. The only catch was that they had question marks embroidered on their collars. He didn't like wearing shirts with question marks on at first – he found it a bit on-the-nose – but got used to it in time and eventually went so far as to knit himself a tank-top with question marks on it too. This was all several thousand years ago when he had more time on his hands.)

'Question marks were nice,' continued Osgood. 'Why don't you wear them any more?'

'I do. I have question mark underpants.'

*Makes one wonder what the question is*, thought Osgood.

The Doctor leaned back in his seat as the plane screeched into the air. He needed to marshal his thoughts. Work out how to defuse this whole situation. He was lacking information and was getting the feeling that he'd been outmanoeuvred. He needed facts.

'So which one are you?' he asked. 'Human or Zygon?'

Osgood looked at him. 'I don't answer that question,' they said softly.

'Why not?'

'Because there is no question to answer, Doctor. I don't accept it. My sister and I were the living embodiment of the peace we made. Imperfect as it might be, I will give as many lives as I have to protect it. You want to know who I am, Doctor? I am the peace.'

'I'm very proud to know you, Osgood. And I promise I won't tell anyone that you're human.'

Osgood looked at him, raising a quizzical eyebrow.

'Zygons need to keep the human original alive to refresh the body print,' the Doctor continued. 'If you were a Zygon, you'd have changed back within days of your sister's death.'

'That's a misunderstanding, Doctor. An oversimplification. Zygons have evolved.'

The Doctor looked up at Osgood. Disquieted. This wasn't something he had known that afternoon in the Black Archive. 'Evolved? In what way?' he asked quietly.

'Zygons only ever needed to keep the original alive if they required more information from them, if they needed access to the subject's brain or memories.'

The Doctor frowned. He didn't quite understand.

'The physical form is a very easy thing to copy,' Osgood continued. 'If it wasn't so straightforward, then we'd never have been able to make so many millions of duplicates at one time and let them disperse around the world.'

'So if it's so easy to make a physical copy, why do you need to keep the original alive at all?'

'Because a purely physical copy isn't a true copy. To make a genuine facsimile, one needs to duplicate the consciousness – the "soul" – of the original. And this is much harder. These things can eventually be downloaded in their entirety, but it takes a long time, and until then we need a live feed.'

'"We"?'

'They.'

The lift came down into the tunnels for the last time. Now fifty UNIT soldiers were assembled in the gloomy tunnel, armed and ready to go. Jac, at the head of the detachment with Clara beside her, walked slowly forward through the blackness and towards the dim red glow that they'd observed earlier. As they moved forward, the tunnel seemed to open outwards more and more. Jac had a sense of space disappearing out around them.

But nobody seemed to be here. She raised her arm softly and the detachment halted. Listened.

A sound in the darkness. A hiss. Clara switched on her torch and turned it towards the sound.

'Hydraulics?' suggested Jac.

Another sound – a squelch – from above. Everyone else switched on their torches and shone them upwards.

Hanging from the ceiling and walls were pods. Human-sized pods. Dangling there amongst slimy fronds and tendrils of Zygon matter.

'Oh my god,' said Jac. She and Clara looked at one another. And then back to the squirming, pulsing pods, moving vaguely like the egg of an almost-hatched insect. Shining their torches further along the cavern, it was clear that there were hundreds of these pods, possibly thousands. They went on as far as torchlight could shine. This was a huge operation.

'You know, I actually think you might be right,' said Clara.

'About what?' asked Jac softly.

Clara went on staring up at the pods. She saw Sandeep. His parents. Everyone from her block of flats. All there. All duplicated. 'About the end of the world.'

The presidential plane flew through the morning sky, heading back home. Inside the meeting room on board, the Zygon who'd been Hitchley's mom – now conscious – sat at the table, its hands bound together. Its eyes darted with minuscule movements, its nostrils flared, scenting the area. It looked quiet, contained, and dangerous.

In its natural state, the Zygon resembled an oversized foetus, with a domed head and curved back. It was greenish-red and covered with suckers. Its eyes were sunken, its mouth a dark maw. Its arms tapered to small hands with a sting in the centre of them which could send a huge electric shock to its prey. Hitchley's mom clenched and unclenched its fists, trying to work free, trying to activate its stinger.

'Okay,' said the Doctor. 'Bit of first-things-firstness.' He sat in the Zygon's line of sight. Beamed at it. 'What's your name?'

No reply.

'My name's – well – you can call me the Doctor. But I suppose you know that. You want something. What is it?'

The Zygon ignored him.

'I'm going to count to five,' said the Doctor. 'Actually, no, I'll count to three. And if you don't tell me what you want by the time I get there – I'm going to let that soldier over there shoot you.'

He gestured towards a UNIT bodyguard standing guard in the doorway.

'One – two – three. All right,' he said, turning to the soldier. 'Shoot it. With your gun.'

'Doctor, you can't,' implored Osgood, as the soldier in the doorway cocked his weapon.

'Course I can. I'll kill a Zygon, no problem. Zygons kill Zygons, Zygons kill humans. Why shouldn't I join in?'

'Because I am already dead,' said the Zygon.

The Doctor looked at the creature. Gestured for the soldier to holster his weapon.

'In fact, Doctor,' continued the Zygon, 'I'm as dead as you are.'

The Doctor considered this for a moment. Then opened his little case of jelly babies and offered one to the creature. 'Since we're both dead, we might as well talk. Jelly baby?'

The Zygon didn't even look at the proffered case. The Doctor offered one to Osgood, who demurred and produced a case of their own.

'You lot. What do you want?' asked the Doctor.

'You're the President of the World?' asked the Zygon.

'Suppose so,' shrugged the Doctor.

It looked at him for a few moments. 'We *want* that world,' it hissed.

'Okay,' said Clara. 'So, it looks like whole building-fulls of people have been pinched. In fact, it looks like a whole London-full of people has been pinched,' she said, flicking her torch up towards the roof, lined with pods.

The troops were readying their weapons as Clara addressed them.

'But we've got them early. They're still growing. And we've got to neutralise these eggs before they hatch. Take your positions.'

The UNIT troops started getting into place to obey the order, to destroy these hideous things. Clara grabbed an assault rifle from one of them and shouldered it.

'I'm enjoying this,' she beamed at Jac.

But Jac was anxious. 'Clara,' she said. Something was playing on her mind but she couldn't quite locate it.

'What?'

'We don't know that's what they are.' Jac shuddered. 'We should wait.'

'Look,' insisted Clara. 'They're *here*. They're growing duplicates of us – we have to destroy them. I've seen it happen – I saw it happen to that little boy. They took his parents and then they took him! Come on. These are . . . Zygon eggs, or whatever – look.'

She ripped aside some of the membrane off the pod she was standing by. Through a translucent patch of membrane, a human face could be seen.

It was *her own face*.

It was the face of Clara Oswald.

Lying there, unconscious, covered in goo and pulsing tendrils.

'Oh, god,' she said, her voice breaking. 'That's *me*.'

She recovered her composure, hefted the gun and looked steadily at Jac. 'We have to destroy these things.'

'But I don't see how these *are* duplicates,' replied Jac, trying to process this. 'That's not how Zygons work – they don't grow duplicates, they kidnap the original, and . . . These have to be the originals in here – these are the humans—'

Jac looked at Clara's pod.

And up to Clara.

Realising.

Too late.

Bonnie looked back at Jac with a vague, cruel smile.

The woman she'd been with all this time was not Clara at all. Bonnie was a convincing Clara, but the facade had now dropped.

Jac backed away. She yelled out to the UNIT troops: 'Retreat! Retreat! This is a trap! It's an ambush!'

The UNIT troops turned. But lined up in front of them in the dark, blocking the exits, were dozens of Zygons. Lined up in an attack formation, shadowy.

'Oh god,' said Jac. 'Open fire!'

The UNIT troops raised their weapons and pulled their triggers. But the guns wouldn't shoot. They were covered in gloop. The guns had been sabotaged. Zygonic pus oozed out from the mechanisms. UNIT had been sent in here, defenceless, to die.

Bonnie crossed the line. She went and stood with the Zygons. Shoulder to shoulder.

'Miss Oswald – please,' sobbed Jac. She begged for her life in vain.

Bonnie looked at the UNIT soldiers. Got out her phone. Started videoing them. 'Execute the traitors,' she ordered.

The Zygons hissed in unison, baring their teeth. And sent out their stings.

With an electrified scream, Jac was reduced to a pile of dust.

The Doctor and Osgood sat opposite the Zygon on the presidential plane.

'We want to be who we are,' it hissed. 'We want to live as ourselves. At any cost. We want a home.'

'Well, you can't have the United Kingdom,' replied the Doctor. 'There's already people living there. They'll think you're going to pinch their benefits.'

'Listen,' said Osgood imploringly. 'We can start again. We made mistakes. You weren't well enough prepared. We can make it work this time. Maybe you can go to the UK, you can try and assimilate yourselves, you can live and work there and take your chances with the rest.'

'We don't want to assimilate,' replied the Zygon coldly. 'We cannot co-exist with the indigenous population of Earth.'

'Well, you can't just get rid of the human race. You can't just take over,' said the Doctor. 'I won't let you.'

'We're already there, Doctor,' said the Zygon. 'The invasion's already taken place. Bit by bit, over the last year. We've won the first battle. And now we're going to start the war.'

Kate and Norlander stood in the entrance of the St James Motel in Truth or Consequences. It was burnt out. Dozens of hairballs here too. The whole town stank of death and corruption.

'There's hundreds more,' said Norlander. 'They killed everyone.'

'We have to find out what forms they took. Whose forms. How many of them there were.' Kate shook her head, aghast at the total failure of the peace that she and Osgood had been in charge of. Why hadn't Jemima and Claudette kept them up to date? Why hadn't they asked for more help? Why hadn't the Doctor been here?

Norlander walked into the hallway, her boots crunching over broken glass.

'How did this happen?' murmured Kate, mostly to herself. Then she peered at Norlander. 'How did you survive? Why didn't you go to the authorities?'

Norlander turned and looked at her.

'How long have you been here on your own?' Kate whispered.

'Someone caught the briefest of glimpses of a Zygon in its proper form,' Norlander said. 'A Zygon child, who hadn't learnt to preserve its body print, who had been left alone to learn these things for itself. To learn everything about this unfamiliar, unfriendly planet alone. And the word went round these primitives that we were monsters.'

Kate felt for her gun. '"We"?' she asked.

'There isn't any back-up, is there?' Norlander flickered, bubbled and spewed a torrent of black, viscous goo out of her mouth as she took her natural form. 'I just had to be sure.'

The creature moved forward in the darkness and lifted its arm. A bolt of electricity shot out towards Kate.

Bonnie, a little dusty and dirty, walked across the floor of the UNIT safehouse. The place seemed empty of personnel, hers to command. There was a crackle on her communications device, and then a voice came through. She recognised it as that of Kate Stewart.

'Commander. UNIT neutralised in North America. Kate Stewart neutralised.'

'Copy that,' replied the Zygon in Clara's shape. 'Remain in her form and return home. Truth or Consequences.'

'Truth or Consequences,' said Kate's voice.

A lone soldier turned the corner in front of her. Bonnie shot out a sting from her wrist and killed him. He dropped to the floor, fizzing into a hairball.

Bonnie nabbed a fearsome-looking bazooka from its shelf and left the room. She entered the main area, crossed to a computer and opened up a program. Taking in the information on the screen for a moment, she raised her communicator and opened a channel to all her operatives.

'Bonnie speaking. UNIT neutralised in the UK. More or less.'

She left the room, shouldering the bazooka.

Open on the desktop of the computer was a flight-tracking program, showing the presidential plane approaching the UK.

'We're just commencing our descent into the UK,' said the pilot. 'Should be landing in about fifteen minutes.'

The Doctor strapped himself in. Not a moment too soon. He needed to get his feet on the ground and start taking control of this messy situation.

'High Commander reports UNIT forces in the UK neutralised,' continued the pilot's voice. 'Truth or Consequences,' it said.

The Doctor jumped back up from his seat. He hurried to the cockpit door. Locked.

Osgood looked across the table at the Zygon. 'This has been a distraction. An ambush. You've just been getting us out of the way.'

'They've been showing us what they're capable of,' said the Doctor.

The Zygon smiled a thin smile. 'All of the UNIT troops are dead,' it said. 'Kate Stewart is dead. The Zygon High Command is dead. There is only you, Doctor. And *that*.' The Zygon gestured to Osgood. 'Everyone who knows about this – everyone who could stop this – is gone.'

'What about the peace treaty?' asked Osgood. 'What was wrong with abiding by the peace treaty? It was there to stop people getting *hurt*.'

'A peace treaty can only be negotiated if there is a winner, and a loser. You've lost.'

The Doctor's phone rang.

'Say goodbye, Doctor,' whispered the Zygon. 'This plane will never land.'

The Doctor answered the call. Clara. Finally getting back to him. Thank goodness.

'Clara?' he whispered.

*Clara was in the flat on the floor below, watching Daddy go and fetch the Little Boy. Mummy appeared from the shadows too.*

*'We can take him,' said Mummy.*

*Daddy returned with the Little Boy. He was kicking and screaming against his father.*

*'Are you okay—?' asked Clara.*

*Daddy didn't say anything. The Little Boy looked over her shoulder, scared.*

*'Everything's fine,' said Mummy, smiling at Clara.*

*The sound of the Little Boy crying abruptly stopped. Clara looked up.*

*Then Daddy returned. He was a Zygon. He held up his hand and shot an electric sting at Clara. Right into her brain.*

*Clara staggered back from Daddy Zygon and Mummy Zygon. As she lost consciousness, she looked up in terror to see* herself. *Herself, coming into the room.*

*'Hello, Clara,' said herself. 'My name's Bonnie.'*

*And that was the last thing that Clara knew.*

Bonnie stood on the White Cliffs of Dover, next to her motorbike.

'Clara?' said the Doctor through the phone.

Bonnie lifted the handset. 'There you are,' she said, doing her best impression of the Doctor's friend at her most jaunty.

'Thank god you're OK,' said the Doctor. 'Listen—'

Bonnie crouched down, got hold of the bazooka she'd taken from UNIT HQ. Shouldered it. 'You're breaking up,' she shouted.

'The invasion's taken place,' said the Doctor breathlessly. 'You're probably surrounded by Zygons. Get to the TARDIS, get yourself safe. I'll be back in about half an hour. I'm going to think of something, OK—'

'I'm sorry, but Clara's dead,' said Bonnie. 'I killed her.'

Bonnie stood there, planting her feet solidly down, getting the plane in her sights. She could almost hear the Doctor's shock over the phone. She smiled.

'It's your decision, Doctor,' said Bonnie. 'Truth. Or Consequences.'

Her finger hovered over the trigger. It trembled momentarily.

Then she fired the bazooka at the presidential plane.

# Chapter 8

## The Diner Across the Road

*After the long swathe of desert, after many* hours, *came a town. Slowly at first, dwellings.* Houses. *And large cubes of glass and concrete.* Stores. *And more of these vehicles moving along the* highway. *They were called cars.* Automobiles.

*Amongst the documents in her handbag had been a* bus ticket. *The destination marked upon it was TRUTH OR CONSEQUENCES. The same name was emblazoned on a large sign at the point in the highway where the desert dwindled to an end and became replaced by dwellings and stores. Truth or Consequences. This, presumably, was her landfall.*

*The bus slowed to a stop. The doors beeped open, and others got to their feet. Bonnie watched them. Stood. Followed. As she stepped through the door, something hit her. Heat. The temperature outside of the bus was extremely high. The temperature within the bus had been significantly lower and she had calibrated her body accordingly. She staggered a little as her systems corrected themselves.*

*Moisture broke out of her skin and she worried for a moment that she was about to assume her native form. She tried to steady herself against the side of the bus, but the metal was scalding hot and caused an alarming sensation on her flesh.* Pain.

*'Are you okay?' said a voice. It was in a deeper register than her own voice. 'Sorry – are you okay? Can I help?'*

*Bonnie turned in the direction of the voice. There was a man opposite her. She recognised him. Her body felt a tang of electricity. She looked at him. She* knew *him . . . Her brain knew him.*

*He looked at her.*

'It feels that we are associated with one another,' *said Bonnie.* 'I have your image in my mind.'

'Your image is also in my mind,' *he said.* 'It is a residual memory. I expect it to clear shortly.'

*Bonnie evaluated him. He was a young man. Approximately the same age as herself. He had ridden on the bus with her. His hair was dark and so were his eyes. His skin was darker than her own.*

'The designation on my documents is Clyde Orson,' *said the man.*

'My designation is Bonnie O'Dowd,' *she said.*

*She looked at him. A voice in her head whispered* Danny. *And she experienced a rush of something which she thought might be called grief.*

'Danny,' *she said.*

'Clara,' *he said.*

'Bonnie,' *she said.*

'Clyde,' *he replied.*

*They looked at one another. He smiled at her. She looked at him for a few moments and attempted a smile herself. It was a little crooked at first and felt a little more like a sneer.*

*They were two newly born Zygons, freshly off the bus in an unknown land.*

*Without knowing why she did so, she put out her hand. He took it, and they walked off down the street together.*

*The sun was relentless. Her body was not designed to cope with direct heat or sustained sunlight. The environment was inhospitable. Her companion, Clyde, seemed to be suffering too. They needed to find shelter and sustenance of some sort.*

'Diner,' *he said, indicating a building across the street from them.*

*They entered the* diner. *Inside, various humans were seated at wooden boards, consuming dead animal and vegetable matter which was reconstituted before them on plates. Bonnie and Clyde found a vacant position near the window and waited. They did not know the procedure for acquiring the dead animal and vegetable matter. But, for a moment, they just allowed themselves to feel the relief of being in the shade.*

*They looked at one another. Smiled again. The sensation of smiling released pleasing chemicals in their brains. They smiled once more. There was another pleasing sensation that accompanied this. That of chemical attraction and a desire to procreate.*

*Before this could go any further, a female in a blue garment and a white head covering appeared by their table.* 'What can I get you?' *she asked.*

*Bonnie glanced down at a document which bore images of dead animal and vegetable matter. She looked at Clyde.*

*He turned to the female.* 'What . . . is your recommendation?' *he said.*

'Are you British?' *asked the woman.*

*Clyde was unsure how to respond. Bonnie stepped in.*

'We are both extremely British,' *she said.* 'One gets very British after riding on a bus for such a long time.'

*The woman laughed.* 'I love your accent,' *she said.*

'Thank you,' *said Bonnie.* 'I love you too.'

*The woman laughed again.* 'What can I get you?'

'Taco,' *said Clyde.*

*The woman smiled at him, writing this down. Waited.*

*Clyde felt that perhaps he had given insufficient instructions.* 'Pizza,' *he said.* 'Cheeseburger, Ribeye Steak, Fries, Milk, Cola, Beer, Coffee, Wine, Ice Cream, Banoffee Pie –'

*Bonnie put her hand on his. Stop.*

*The woman wrote this down, clearly enjoying the eccentricity of these two exotic creatures. She turned to Bonnie.* 'And for you, miss?'

'Mac and cheese and cheese,' *said Bonnie.* 'And cheese.'

*The woman nodded and walked away.*

'What are our orders?' *asked Clyde.*

'I do not know,' *said Bonnie.*

*A man was banging at the window next to them. He was the driver of the bus, and he looked agitated. He was trying to attract their attention. They looked at him. He shook his head and entered the restaurant.*

'You left your bags!' *he said in a loud voice.* 'Why would you leave your bags? I don't have time to deal with calling in a bomb scare. Take your things with you, okay?'

'Bags?' *said Clyde.*

'They're there on the street. Have a good day,' *said the driver, and then he was gone.*

*Clyde got up from his seat and went into the sun. There were some receptacles there on the dusty road. He wheeled them back to the diner and placed them on their table. Perhaps their instructions were to be found within.*

WELCOME TO PLANET EARTH, *said the card.*

This is your home. This is where you were hatched.

*Bonnie and Clyde read their cards together.*

You are a child of the Zygon race but you are destined to take refuge amongst humans. Your assimilation and integration is key to your survival. Humanity does not know you are here.

*Bonnie frowned. Did the waitress and the bus driver*

*not know that she was here? Why then had they spoken to her?*

As you grow, you will find that you can assume your natural shape. You must never do this within sight of a human being. You must suppress your identity. Live the life that has been chosen for you. Fit in. It is vital that you try to fit in. Otherwise, terrible consequences will ensue. Do not attempt to make contact with High Command. We will issue further instructions as necessary.

*That was it. Bonnie turned the card around to see if there was anything written on the back. But there was nothing.*

*Inside the bag were some bundles of paper with mysterious symbols. There was a collection of garments and implements which looked as though they were designed to maintain aspects of the human body. But nothing else.*

'We have been abandoned by our Skarasen,' *said Bonnie.*

*Clyde reached his hand around the array of plates and cups which the waitress had brought them.*

'We have one another,' *he said.*

# Chapter 9

# The Creature in the Dream

Blackness. The Doctor's voice on the phone.

'Clara – Clara – CLARA—'

But Clara was in a pod, in the Zygon Cavern. Clara's eyes were closed. Clara was asleep.

'There you are,' said Bonnie over the phone.

Voices on a phone line.

Clara was stuck in her pod. Stuck there, on the sticky, sickly wall. The pod had moulded itself completely around her body. Her face was three-quarters covered with the tendrils and the polyps and the messy Zygon junk. Suffocating.

'Thank god you're okay, Clara. Listen—' said the Doctor's voice over the phone.

His last words echoed and sharpened.

'Thank god you're okay, Clara. Listen—'

Who was having this phone conversation that she could hear?

Clara's eyes moved, REM like, under the lids.

'Thank god you're okay, Clara. Listen—'

The Doctor was talking to Clara. Clara was okay . . . But *she* was Clara. And she was *not* okay . . . And she wasn't talking to the Doctor.

'Listen – listen – LISTEN!' said the Doctor. His voice echoing through the dark.

In her bedroom, Clara sat up in bed with a jolt. Awake. Alert.

She looked around herself, breathing heavily, anxious. Had she had a nightmare? She remembered no details. Just a feeling of smothering suffocation. A sensation of *ugh*. She picked up her phone from the bedside table next to her. No one had called. No one had texted.

Clara checked the time. 6:P6am. *What?*

She put down the phone, frowned, then picked it up and checked the time again: 6:26am. But she was sure it had just said 6:P6am. There was no such time as 6:P6. What kind of time was that supposed to be? P-ty-six minutes past six. Clara sat there for a moment, unable to shake the idea that something was badly wrong and about to get worse.

It was still dark in the flat, all the curtains and blinds were drawn. There was the sound of a plane approaching; distant as yet but growing louder.

She got out of bed and crossed the room sluggishly. She checked the rest of the flat. The TV was on in the living room, white noise fizzing away on it . . . Why was there white noise? Did TVs even still have white noise? She didn't know. What was the noise of that plane?

She went into the bathroom. At the sink, she glanced at herself in the mirror and dabbed a strand of yesterday's mascara off her cheek. As she did so, vague noises started coming through the white noise on the TV.

Why hadn't she turned the TV off when she was in there?

The sound of the plane became gradually louder and louder. The plane was coming nearer and nearer.

Clara opened the bathroom cabinet and took out her toothbrush and toothpaste. The writing on the tube was blurred. Indistinct. She held it up to see it better. Perhaps she needed glasses. As she looked, it came into focus. It read: THIS IS TOOTHPASTE.

She looked down at it, frowning. Did toothpaste usually describe itself in this fashion? She squeezed the tube out onto her toothbrush. It was not toothpaste at all, despite its claims. It was hideous dirty green gloop. She dropped the toothbrush, disgusted. It landed on the sink. The toothpaste on the brush was clean and white and normal now. Clara peered down at it. THIS IS TOOTHPASTE. A noise came through from the TV in the living room.

'You're breaking up.' It was Clara's voice. Her own voice.

A phone conversation again. Clara was talking, replying.

But *she* was Clara.

Clara left the bathroom and hurried to the TV. There was an image of an approaching aeroplane, as seen from the ground. The picture faded, distorted, then came back into vision and focus again. A point-of-view shot of a plane in the sky, gradually descending on its approach to land.

'The invasion's taken place,' said the Doctor. 'You're probably surrounded by Zygons. Get to the TARDIS, get yourself safe. I'll be back in about half an hour.'

Why was the Doctor talking on the phone on her television? And what was he talking about? *Zygons*. She remembered something about Zygons.

And when was he coming? Half an hour? When was half an hour? 6:S6?

'I'm sorry, but Clara's dead,' said her own voice on the television. 'I killed her.'

Clara took a sudden intake of breath. The TV cut to white noise again. Starting to get extremely anxious now, she grabbed her phone from where she had left it by the bed. Scrolled through and found THE DOCTOR. She pressed his number. The screen didn't respond. She pressed it again. No response. Again, again, again. This was like a nightmare.

She looked down at her phone. It seemed very far away. It was out of battery, powering down. The noise of the approaching plane became louder, louder, more urgent. A whine in the tone of its engines sounded as though something was wrong.

Clara thought for a moment. 'Get to the TARDIS,' he'd said. 'Get yourself safe.' She hurried down the hallway to her front door.

But it wasn't there.

Just a blank patch of wall where the front door should be, where it usually was. The blank patch was the same colour as the rest of the walls. Everything around the door – coat-hangers, keys on a hook – was as it should be. Just a well-camouflaged bald spot in the place from which the door had taken leave. She couldn't get out.

The lights in the flat flickered.

In the Zygon Cavern, Clara's eyes flickered beneath her eyelids.

Clara looked at the non-existent door for a moment, then went to the window and opened the curtains. But there was no window there either: just wall. Curtains on a rail above. A windowsill with pot plants and stuff. But just a perfectly smooth wall where the window should be.

Clara reasoned that the only sensible explanation for this whole crazy situation with the doors and windows was that she must still be asleep.

She'd got stuck in a dream before and she knew that there were ways out of it, ways to tell.

'Dream-checks . . . dream-checks . . .' she whispered to herself.

She picked up a newspaper sitting on the table. She knew that one of the ways to interrogate a dream was to ask it to provide details. The headline was just a jumble of irrelevant words: IPQUE SSL VELP KJKK, with a picture of a seahorse. She pored over the text underneath – nonsense, nonsense, just the usual dreamlike vaguely realised nonsense – until, suddenly, something made her stop.

**It's your decision, Doctor.**

On the plane, the Doctor was almost frantic. She could hear the shock in his voice.

'Clara – CLARA!'

At the same time that Clara read it in the newspaper, she heard it through the television. Her own voice: 'It's your decision, Doctor.'

Clara withdrew a little. Turned the pages. The headline on the back page, startlingly, read: **Truth. Or Consequences.**

'Truth. Or Consequences,' said her own voice on the TV.

Clara swung round.

*

On the screen was the point-of-view shot. The sights of some sort of weapon, lining up with the plane. It was the presidential plane. It was the Doctor's plane. The sights locked onto it. Whoever it was was going to blow him up.

Clara whacked the TV, jolting it.

On the cliff edge, just as Bonnie fired her bazooka, it jolted to one side.

Someone had shoved her arm.

The Doctor and Osgood were on the presidential plane. The Doctor was almost frantic, still talking on the phone: 'Clara – CLARA!'

Osgood noticed something, pointed through the window. 'Doctor—'

The missile from Bonnie's bazooka whizzed past. The plane banked sharply.

The Doctor looked up. 'Missed!'

There was a loud CRUMP as the shell exploded in mid-air, many metres wide of the plane.

Clara's flat jolted as the missile burst in the sky.

Bonnie stood on the White Cliffs of Dover, holding her bazooka, standing by the motorbike. She was reloading the weapon. Settling in for a second go. The plane was turning. She wouldn't have more than one more chance.

In her flat, Clara watched the sights centre on the plane again. She slammed the side of the telly. But this time it was rock solid, it wouldn't move.

Bonnie's legs were firmly planted on the ground. She was braced against the side of her motorcycle. Calm and steady, her finger curled round the trigger, cueing up her second attempt . . .

Clara slammed the television again: no effect. She thought frantically, *What, what? What can I do?*

Bonnie's finger tensed on the trigger . . .

Clara looked at her hand, forming into trigger-pull position, like she was sensing the outside world, like the muscles of her hand were being controlled and contracted by someone else. Was she about to pull the trigger? Then she bit her own trigger finger, hard.

Bonnie's finger trembled over the bazooka trigger, sensing a sudden pain. Then, with steely effort, she controlled herself, took possession of her finger and fired. The missile whooshed off into the sky, towards its distant target.

Bonnie looked in her wing mirror. Saw her reflection.

She could feel that there was somebody there. Someone waking in her brain.

She glanced up at the plane in the sky and the missile slowly approaching.

She looked coldly at her reflection and smiled. 'What did you think of that, Clara Oswald?'

With a colossal explosion, the missile hit the aircraft and it blew into a million pieces.

# Chapter 10

## The Man on the Estate

There was something different about London. He had sensed it this morning when he awoke.

Some change in the underlying current of the city. It was hard to put one's tentacle on what it was.

Human society is a mess of contrasting noises and moods. The sounds of transport and music, of footsteps, laughter, argument and shopping. Of televisions burbling and meals being prepared. The quiet of a church and the loudness of a pub. In London, billions of these sounds and feelings bustled endlessly together and give a sensation that one can recognise as the life of a city. But today it felt different. It was quiet, calm. There was no sense of disparate things happening at random. Everything felt ordered. Everything felt the same. London looked like it was supposed to look. But it felt and sounded different. It felt as though it was waiting. It felt as though it was an impersonation of itself.

Etoine hurried along.

He was in the housing estate where he had lived

since he was hatched. Although he had the physical appearance of a man in late middle age, he was only, in fact, about eighteen months old. He had been snatched away from the milk of his Skarasen before he could remember. Scarcely even a child and here he was, fending for himself in the middle of an alien jungle.

He carried a shopping bag. There were baked beans in it. Humans often carried such totems. He had yet to work out why humans needed to carry so much with them at all times. Communications devices, tokens to be given in exchange for materials, images of their Skarasens, things having to do with their reproductive cycle and their physical wellbeing. He often examined the things that humans took with them and could rarely work out the meaning of them.

He hurried past a street-sweeper who was brooming some stuff across the pavement and collided with the man, spilling his shopping on the pavement. The street-sweeper looked sternly at him. Etoine didn't apologise. He thought about picking up the beans for a moment, but merely hurried on. Etoine wasn't sure who the man was. He didn't get a *human* feeling from him. The street-sweeper watched him go. He picked up the rubbish he was sweeping and put it in his little bin truck.

Etoine had the feeling he was being followed.

Etoine.

He had liked that name. There was nobody with that name. It was random, he knew, which name you got. Whose face, which body. But he liked his name. He liked his face.

He liked his dwelling. The view over the tall green plants. He liked the place downstairs where one exchanged one's tokens for nourishment in different containers. Eventually he had worked out that one was not supposed to eat cat food. It did not contain cats but was meant for them to consume. He had felt safe amongst all these others, who looked more or less like him.

But something had increasingly felt wrong recently. There was some anger in the species field. Something was brewing.

The High Command had gone silent. Nothing was certain.

The concept of 'uncertainty' was not one that he'd understood until long after he'd come here. It was something that he'd had to learn from watching the behaviour of others. Watching them when they interacted with one another and went about their daily lives. Uncertainty was a 'feeling'. A feeling that he had no equivalent for.

But the strange thing was, that the longer one lived in these bodies, the more one began to understand. About their 'feelings'. About things such as happiness. Love. Sadness. Contentment. All sorts of things that he had never had a word for before, nor any need for such a word.

It was as if these things were part of the physical fabric of being a person. And Etoine found that fascinating. He liked it. And he liked his name.

A message burst through into his brain from the control polyp. *The invasion has begun. You will face a choice. Truth or Consequences.*

He didn't know what this could mean. This message could not be from the two little girls. Something had gone wrong.

Huffing and puffing, Etoine staggered through the low-rise blocks and the graffiti to his dilapidated flat and turned his key in the lock. Inside, it was cluttered with junk, uncleaned, barely furnished. He hurried to his kitchen table, where a very old laptop, repaired with sticky tape, sat buzzing quietly to itself.

Etoine booted it up. The screen came on, and he pressed the Z button on the keyboard. It was more worn than all the rest. He pushed the button, harder, more insistently – Z Z Z Z Z – until gloop started to seep out from around it. This was the emergency protocol for getting in touch with his commanders.

Unlike some of the others, he had been kept here in England as a lieutenant for the High Command. He had been made aware of this after a few months of living alone and fending for himself. He had been visited by two little girls who began to give him missions. He hated doing it, he hated carrying out their orders. Sometimes he was commanded to neutralise other

Zygons. Zygons who were not obeying the ceasefire. He had been an executioner.

There was a knock on the door.

Etoine turned with a start. He walked softly along the hallway. Peered through the peephole. Nervous.

He saw a young human woman with dark hair and red lipstick standing there. He leant back against the wall, trying not to breathe. She would go away if she didn't think he was here.

Then the door started to unlock from the other side. Etoine recoiled, backing down the hall.

The door opened.

Bonnie stood there.

'I know what you are . . .' she said.

Etoine looked at her for a moment.

'I –'

Bonnie moved closer to him. 'I know what they've made you do. But I'm not going to punish you. I'm going to set you free.'

Etoine recoiled in horror. Bonnie looked at him. Cold. Ruthless. She advanced.

'Please. Please,' begged Etoine.

'Humans cannot accept us the way we really are. If we cannot hide, we must surely fight. You're going to be the first. You're going to be the first to make the humans see.'

Etoine didn't answer.

Bonnie reached up, putting her hands on either side

of his head. She delivered a bolt of electricity to him. He staggered back. Took his chance and bolted to the door. He hurried outside.

Inside the flat, Bonnie tapped on Etoine's computer. There were a number of encoded files there, from the Zygon High Command.

She clicked on the one that she was looking for. It was called *In The Event Of The Ceasefire Breaking Down.*

It was a video file.

Etoine tumbled down the steps and ran across the courtyard of his estate. Panicking. Something was happening to him. He lifted his hand up. It was blistering. Green and red blisters breaking out on it. He was transforming into a Zygon.

*'Hello,' said the two Osgoods on screen.*

*'Operation Double – The Zygon Peace Treaty,' they said in unison, adjusting their glasses.*

*'I am Osgood,' said the first.*

*'I am also Osgood,' said the second. 'Remember that. It'll be important later.'*

Bonnie watched.

Etoine staggered past a bunch of kids sitting on a wall. He turned to them, waving his hand dumbly, desperately. His alien flesh was breaking out all over his body.

'Help me! Help me!'

The kids watched. Even with his limited knowledge of human behaviour, he could tell that they were weirdly nonreactive. Were they Zygons, too? Or just unfazed by anything? Were they to do with *her*?

Above, Bonnie emerged from his flat and came to the edge of the walkway. She stood looking down at Etoine. She lifted up her phone, and videoed it.

'HELP ME!' Etoine's voice echoed around the estate. He staggered towards shelter. Into the shopping centre across the way.

Bonnie lowered her phone. Smiled. Brought up her communicator.

'Commander here. The first one has been changed. I'm going to UNIT to retrieve the Osgood Box.'

(In her dream apartment, Clara sat cross-legged on the floor.

She was concentrating hard. One hand was extended in front of her, as if she was miming texting. Her thumb moved slowly and deliberately over an imaginary phone . . .)

As Bonnie headed along the walkway and down to her car, her phone was still held loosely in her hand.

Oblivious to herself, Bonnie's thumb moved slowly

across the surface of her phone, bringing up the text message box.

(Clara's eyes were still shut. She was visualising this, seeing what Bonnie was seeing, feeling what she was feeling. She was thumbing a text into an imaginary phone. She started to smile.

It was working!)

The low tide lapped over a rocky beach, somewhere on the south coast of England.

The water was bringing in odd bits of debris. Bits of aeroplane.

A seat sat tipped up in the water. An engine. And a large Union Jack parachute was spread half over the sand and half in the sea.

Osgood sat up amongst it, suddenly snapping into consciousness, wet and dishevelled. They looked for their glasses and found them snapped in half at their side.

They stood up, squinting first through one lens and then the other. Looking around for any sign of the—

'Doctor!' Osgood yelled.

'Any questions?' he said.

Osgood turned. The Doctor stood there, a few metres away, calmly unclipping his parachute from his back. His Union Jack parachute.

Osgood dazedly took all this in. They could find no

sensible questions to ask, apart from: 'Why do you have a Union Jack parachute?'

'Camouflage,' he said.

'Camouflage?'

'Yes. Camouflage. We're in Britain.'

The Doctor splashed over to Osgood's side, dusting the sand and seaweed from himself, and looked at his friend with concern. 'You've broken your specs,' he said. 'Here, let me fix them.'

He took Osgood's glasses and examined them briefly. Then threw them away.

'No, they're knackered. Have mine instead. They're sonic.'

'Sonic specs?' Osgood asked.

'Yeah,' said the Doctor, who clearly thought that this was a cool idea.

'Isn't that a bit pointless?' Osgood wondered. 'Like having – I dunno – a visual hearing-aid?'

'What's wrong with pointless?' said the Doctor, looking hurt. 'I once invented an invisible watch. Spot the design flaw.'

'Ah,' nodded Osgood. 'You're talking nonsense to distract me from being scared. It's one of your known character traits.' They put the glasses on.

'Don't look at my browser history,' the Doctor muttered.

Osgood recoiled as they put the glasses on. 'Whoa—!'

'I said, *Don't.*'

Having expected to be dead, Osgood had not made any plans for what to do next. 'Why didn't that Zygon blow us up with her big bazooka?' they asked.

'She did blow us up with her big bazooka,' replied the Doctor. 'This is us being blown up with a big bazooka.'

'But I mean, she seems to know what she's doing. The first thing I'd do if I wanted to invade the world would be to kill you.'

'Thanks.'

'I wouldn't even let you get talking. You always get talking. And it's fatal. If I really wanted my plan to succeed, I'd put a bullet between your eyes, first thing.'

'Again, thanks.' The Doctor put out his hand to help Osgood over a slippery piece of rock. 'Really thought this through, haven't you?'

'I'm a big fan. But listen: my point is, she gave you a chance to get out. She hesitated. I think maybe Clara's still in there, somewhere. Maybe she's not dead.'

The Doctor was pointedly silent, he didn't reply. It took Osgood a moment to get it. Osgood was always a step or two behind when it came to reading the feelings of others. Even before the whole Zygon thing, this had always been an issue.

'You've gone quiet because I mentioned Clara, and you think she *is* dead.'

The Doctor sighed. 'Maybe. I don't know,' he replied.

'I'm trying to hold on to the "hope" phase.' He continued hurrying up the cliffs.

Osgood followed. 'Why do they want to destroy the ceasefire?' they said.

'Don't think of them as if they're rational,' the Doctor replied. 'They're not. They don't care about human beings, and they don't care about their own people. They think the rest of Zygonkind are traitors. They're a splinter group.'

'But they must be doing it for a reason—'

'Splinters,' mused the Doctor. 'Little, unpleasant things that stick under the surface and cause infection. Tiny, insignificant things that inflict a degree of pain which is entirely disproportionate to their size.'

'What's the next move?'

The Doctor's phone beeped in his pocket. He took it out.

It was a message. From CLARA.

The Doctor stopped dead.

'Clara,' said Osgood confusedly.

'No. The Zygon who killed her.' The Doctor tossed Osgood the phone. 'Read it.'

Osgood squinted through the unaccustomed sonic spectacles. 'It says, "I'm awake."'

'What does she mean, she's awake? Politically? A political awakening? Why would she send me propaganda? She just blew me up with a bazooka.'

Osgood took the phone back and stared at the message. Something started to dawn.

'It's not from the Zygon,' they said. 'It actually *is* from Clara.'

'She's dead,' grunted the Doctor.

'No. She's in a pod somewhere. Someone as valuable as Clara – someone with so much knowledge – there's no way they would risk killing her. They need a live feed to the information in her brain. It would take months for them to download it all.'

The Doctor raised an eyebrow at Osgood.

'I know how this works, Doctor,' said Osgood. 'And it goes *both ways*. If you keep the live link active for a long time, then the two personalities start to merge. You can't help it. Clara's fighting back – trying to take control, piece by piece.'

'By texting me?'

Osgood handed the Doctor his phone back. 'The Zygon probably doesn't even know it sent this. Or why it delayed firing that bazooka.'

The Doctor staring down at the thumbnail of Clara which beamed down over the text message. Hardly daring to believe. 'It's just a theory,' he said. 'You don't *know*.'

'Yeah, it's just a theory. But how's the hope phase now?'

'Worse than ever.'

'Then we've got a game!'

Osgood reached the foot of some steps up to the promenade above the cliffs. And bounded up them, two at a time.

Bonnie arrived back at the UNIT safehouse and went into Osgood's office. There was a safe in the back wall, hidden under a photograph of Osgood's father, who had also been known as Osgood.

As Bonnie headed to the safe, she caught her reflection in a mirror. And as she passed, it stuck her tongue out at her.

Bonnie stopped. Backed up. Peered in at the mirror. Moved her right hand.

The reflection moved its left hand.

And winked at her.

Fury flickered across Bonnie's face. 'No!'

She punched the mirror, hard. And the glass shattered.

(In her pod, Clara spasmed, as if responding to the impact, going limp.)

Bonnie went to the safe and keyed in the code that Osgood had given up during interrogation in Turmezistan. She pulled open the door and frowned. Inside, there was no box. Just a laptop computer. Bonnie checked the safe. Nothing else there, save for a half-eaten bag of jelly babies.

Bonnie put the laptop on Osgood's desk and flipped it open. The only file on the desktop was another video clip.

Bonnie growled softly. And played it.

'Hello,' beamed Osgood 1, on the clip. 'If you're watching this, I have been captured and interrogated.'

'During the interrogation, I have revealed to you all the information I know. You have seen my last video about the existence of the Osgood Box,' said Osgood 2.

'I have revealed its location and the combination to open this safe.'

'And guess what?'

'I lied,' said the two Osgoods.

Bonnie sneered. She was getting sick of these two.

'The Osgood Box exists,' said Osgood 1.

'But it's not here. And we don't know where it is,' said Osgood 2.

'The Osgood Box can end the ceasefire,' said #1.

'The Osgood Box can start the war,' said #2.

'But there's a reason it's called the Osgood Box. Haven't you guessed?'

Two impish smiles. And the picture flickered out.

Bonnie hammered her hand against the table. Roared in a guttural, Zygon way. Grabbed the laptop and flung it to the ground and stamped on it until the image of the two irritating Osgoods died in her mind.

Clara's phone buzzed in her pocket.

Bonnie jumped.

It was from THE DOCTOR.
A video call.

'Are they here for us?' asked Osgood.

A police car was waiting on the promenade at the top of the cliffs, its lights flashing. There were two officers in it, watching the Doctor and Osgood. They made no sign of movement.

Osgood had the Doctor's phone clamped to their ear. Nobody was answering.

The policemen looked at them. The Doctor looked back. The policeman in the driver's seat wound down his window. The Doctor showed his psychic paper.

'Doctor John Disco. It was my plane.'

The policeman didn't say anything. Osgood watched him suspiciously. 'Doctor—' they said.

'I had a big plane,' continued the Doctor, 'for purposes of poncing about. Just went off with a massive bang about half a mile that way.'

No reaction. The Doctor and Osgood exchanged glances. Something was off about these two.

'You know what?' smiled Osgood. 'Actually, we're fine – aren't we?'

'Yeah,' said the Doctor. 'So you can just – move along.'

He took Osgood's hand and they hurried off down the street. Glancing back, Osgood saw one of the police officers raise a communication device and mutter a few words. A couple of seconds later, the police car turned around and started to pursue them.

At the UNIT safehouse, Bonnie accepted the call. 'Yes?'

'She's answered!' said Osgood.

The Doctor held up the phone as he jogged along. 'Hello!' he said.

'You're dead,' said Bonnie on the screen, unsettled.

The Doctor glanced behind. The police car was speeding up in their direction. 'Indeed. And I might be even more dead in a minute. You seem to have people everywhere.'

He noticed a car park across the road. 'Nab some wheels,' he said to Osgood.

He and Osgood headed to the cars.

'Van. Specs. Setting 137,' said the Doctor, nodding to a white van parked nearby. Osgood got busy stealing the vehicle and the Doctor held up his phone, peering at the copy of Clara who was addressing him.

'So – what's your plan, Zygella?'

'I don't have a plan,' said Bonnie.

'Come on, you don't invade planets without a plan. That's why they're called planets. To remind you to plan-it, yeah?' The Doctor laughed to himself. 'That was a good one, right? Puntastic! Doctor Puntastic!'

Osgood opened the van and climbed in. The Doctor

clambered into the passenger seat. The police car stopped at the entrance to the car park, blocking their way. Osgood reversed. Behind them, another couple of policemen appeared, standing at the other exit to the car park.

'Don't you want to destroy the oil industry by floating the Loch Ness Monster up the River Thames?' continued the Doctor. 'Or disrupt the course of history by hiding in the National Gallery and pretending to be Queen Elizabeth I?'*

'Why would I want to do that?'

'Because it's a plan! Come on, Zygella, play the game!'

Osgood took a deep breath, revved the engine of the van and screamed towards the two policemen. The van knocked each of them flying and, as it accelerated off down the road, Osgood saw a brief flash of two greeny-red Zygons, staggering and collapsing where the policemen had been. The Doctor glanced at Osgood, impressed.

'The game's changed,' said the woman on his phone. 'And don't call me Zygella. My name's Bonnie.'

Bonnie winked at him.

The Doctor frowned. 'And you're winking at me.'

---

* See DOCTOR WHO AND THE LOCH NESS MONSTER and DOCTOR WHO AND THE DAY OF THE DOCTOR

'I'm not winking at you. Where is the Osgood Box?'

(In the Zygon Cavern, Clara's eye winked.)

At the UNIT safehouse, Bonnie winked again at the Doctor.

'You do know what winking means?' he said. 'You're sending some very serious mixed ones. You know I'm 2,000 years old, right? I mean, I'm old enough to be your Messiah.'

'I am not winking at you,' she insisted, starting to lose her composure. 'I'll ask you one more time. Where is the box?'

Bonnie winked. She could feel herself winking, but she was unable to do anything to stop it. 'Tell me!' she demanded.

The Doctor looked at her for a moment. 'Okay. Non-verbal communication,' he said. 'I imagine you never bothered to learn Morse code. Okay, well, it's going to have to be twenty questions. What else can you do other than wink? Can you fart?'

'Fart?' hissed Bonnie.

(In the Zygon pod, Clara's face smiled vaguely.)

'Where's your pod, Clara?' said the Doctor, becoming serious. 'A tunnel?'

Bonnie winked. She clasped her hand over her eye.

The Doctor hazarded a guess, remembering the maps he'd seen in the training camp in Turmezistan. 'The River Fleet?'

Bonnie winked with the other eye. Angrily, she placed her hand over both eyes.

'Stay where you are, Clara. We're coming to get you. For god's sake, don't tell her where the Osgood Box is, and above all, don't tell her *what* it is.'

With that, the Doctor hung up.

The van hurtled out of town and up towards a motorway junction. 'Obviously the Zygon could hear that?' said Osgood.

'Obviously,' replied the Doctor.

'So she's going to start poking around inside Clara's mind, looking for answers.'

The Doctor beamed at Osgood. 'The mind of Clara Oswald. She may never find her way out!'

'I don't think I've ever seen you smile before.'

'Dazzling, isn't it?'

A plan was coming together.

Something came through on the sonic specs. Osgood glanced at it as they drove. 'There's a ping on Clara's phone – Bonnie's phone, I mean. She uploaded a video from an estate in South London.'

The Doctor watched. It showed Etoine stumbling across the courtyard of his estate, morphing back and forth between his human and Zygon forms, crying out in pain. It cut to black and was replaced by the words

TRUTH OR CONSEQUENCES. The video had been uploaded to all the social media channels. The Doctor winced. This needed to be put back in its box as soon as possible.

'Why Truth or Consequences?' asked Osgood.

'Because, I think they want people to deal with the truth or face the consequences.'

'So what's the truth?' murmured Osgood.

'That there are twenty million Zygons living here.'

'And what are the consequences?'

'God knows. Okay,' said the Doctor, stealing a piece of chewing gum from a packet on the dashboard. 'London: perpetual city, cradle of culture – here we come. Clara, stay safe.'

Bonnie had had enough of this. It was time to demonstrate exactly who was in charge.

'He's coming to get you,' she said to the girl in the broken mirror.

She crushed a fragment of the mirror beneath her heel.

'But guess what? So – am – I.'

# Chapter 11

## The Motel on the Edge of Town

*Time had passed. Time was a human concept. Like the soul.*

*It was unfamiliar to feel time passing. Bonnie sensed that Zygons did not measure time or feel it in their bodies in the way that humans did. Eons and light years could pass for Zygons without notice. Seasons and planetary movements did not impact their functioning. Humans had evolved around the orbits of the Earth and the cycles of the sun. They were ensnared in the mechanisms of the clocks that they had created. They marked every second and every minute and built the structures of their lives around them. For Bonnie, this was very uncomfortable. It felt like being trapped amongst thorns. The ticking of these clocks felt like the burrowing of a beetle in her brain.*

*Months had passed.*

*She and Clyde had left the diner after dining that first day. For a while, they'd believed that they were meant to live there and had remained at their tables all through the long afternoon and the dark evening, until the friendly waitress became unfriendly and asked them to pay up and go. They did not know what 'paying up' entailed. The waitress became even more unfriendly and summoned a man, who shouted at them. They realised that they were expected to exchange some of the pieces of paper in their bags for the food that they had been given. They did so and went out into the cold night.*

*Bonnie and Clyde had needed to find shelter. The terrible heat had given way to a chilly cold. They walked through the town and found a door unlocked. There they rested beneath a large vehicle until a man found them in the morning and chased them away.*

*They wandered the streets the next day, becoming dusty and dirty. They tried to get into the diner once again, but the angry man whom the friendly waitress had summoned told them they were no longer welcome. They needed to escape the sun and went along, trying any door that they came to, until a woman in a car marked* POLICE *came and stopped them.*

*Bonnie remembered seeing that word.* POLICE.

*A phrase had come into her mind at that moment. A fragment of information from that locked room.* POLICE BOX.

*What did it mean? What was inside a police box?*

*The woman in the car marked* POLICE *came out and talked to them. She told them that they were causing concern. She asked whether they were vagrants. They told her that they needed shelter.*

*'You're British,' she said with an impatient voice. 'So many British here all of a sudden.'*

*'Yes, we are very British,' said Bonnie. 'We have not had our breakfast.'*

*'There's a motel just out of town. That's where the British are,' said the POLICE woman. She considered them for a moment. 'Get in. I'll drive you.'*

*They had arrived at a decrepit building on the edges of the desert.*

*There were others there. Living in that building. Others of their own kind. Children of the hatchery. Like them. Like Bonnie and Clyde.*

*The Zygons of Earth.*

*Alone, abandoned and confused.*

*Life was not straightforward at the motel.*

*The others who had come had worked out some of the rules that were necessary to survive here. But they did not know enough. Many important things from the brains and memories of the humans whose forms they had taken were blocked from them. It made survival and adaptation very difficult.*

*Soon, the currency from the luggage ran out. It was exchanged for food, or it was stolen by opportunistic humans.*

*Some of the Zygons at the motel attempted to find employment. This would give them access to more currency. But employment was not easy to come by. The humans were not disposed to be helpful. They would not give their employment to these 'British' people who had taken up residence on the edge of their town. Truth or Consequences was its name.*

*Some of the Zygons at the motel attempted to find help and assistance from the police. They were given none. They attempted to extract currency from the government, but the procedures were complex and nobody seemed to fully understand them. They decided to try and contact High Command. They sent out a telepathic message but the only answer that came back was* BE SILENT. ASSIMILATE.

*Some of the Zygons tried to leave town. But most of them eventually straggled back, unable to cope in the desert on their own.*

*At this time, some of the Zygons discovered alcohol and other such substances. They found that the consumption of these substances had a deadening effect on the chemical anxieties that the community increasingly struggled with. But these substances impacted badly on their bodies and brains and made them behave recklessly.*

*The problem of the locked room in her mind began to occupy Bonnie more and more as she and the other Zygons found themselves unable to go outside. She had feelings about what it contained. Inside was* Clara. *Inside was* Danny. *Inside were* Doctor *and* POLICE BOX.

*She considered this. She asked Clyde.*

*He said that there were memories in his mind. He said that his shape was that of a man called* Danny. *He had loved a woman called* Clara, *whose features corresponded with those of Bonnie. They had lived in London.*

*'Do you have a locked room in your mind?' she asked.*

*He shrugged. He did not know.*

*'I have a locked room in my mind. It contains* Doctor.*'*

*Clyde searched his memories. 'My mind also contains* Doctor. Doctor *is associated with* Clara. Doctor *travels in* POLICE BOX.*'*

*'Who is* Doctor*?' she asked.*

*'*Doctor *is not human,' said Clyde, frowning. '*Doctor *is alien.* Danny's *memories do not contain favourable emotions towards* Doctor. Doctor *is bad.'*

*Bonnie considered this. 'When I think of this locked room in my mind, I receive an impression that* Doctor *is involved with Zygons. I receive an impression that* Doctor *is to blame for sending us to this place.'*

*'How?' asked Clyde.*

*'I don't know,' she replied. 'I cannot unlock the door.'*

*As they grew and matured, the Zygons at the motel experimented with changing form. It was very difficult for them, as if they had been somehow locked into the human shapes in which they had arrived. It was not natural to be so locked into a shape. It was unhealthy. It led to assimilation and cross-contamination. So they tried to break through.*

*They experimented with breaking into the few memories that they could harvest from their human counterparts, and found themselves able to make brief, imperfect facsimiles of the persons contained therein. They began to rifle within their host minds and mine any and all useful information. And, after much practice, they found themselves able to morph into their original forms.*

*One day, Clyde cried out in agony and was unable to maintain his form. His human counterpart was dying, and this was very painful for him. Bonnie nursed him as much as possible but, after that, it was as though a light had gone out. He became cold with her, as though he no longer knew her. He started joining those Zygons who went out to the diner and consumed alcohol. She would wait for him to return, anxious and concerned. It was dangerous to go out. The humans had started to hunt them. Often, fewer Zygons came back than left the motel.*

*On the final evening, the others brought Clyde back home. After ingesting alcohol in the diner, he had staggered into the street and accidentally shifted shape into his true form. For a moment he became a Zygon and not a human. He was observed mid-transformation and beaten by the humans. He was dying of his injuries and unable to speak. He just held her hand and looked mournfully at Bonnie before slipping away.*

*That night, the townspeople surrounded the motel. The Zygons were trapped inside. The humans became violent. But the Zygons fought back.*

*This was the beginning of the end.*

*

*The trauma of watching Clyde die had sent shockwaves through Bonnie's brain.*

*The door of the locked room was suddenly open. There were people inside.*

*'Any second now,' said one of them, 'you're going to stop that countdown. Both of you. Together.'*

*There was a* clock. *One of those irritating devices that caused so much discomfort to her. 00:51, it said. Which meant less than a minute. A short space of time.*

*'And then,' said another one of the people in the room, 'you're going to negotiate the most perfect peace treaty of all time.'*

*'Safeguards all round,' said the first person. 'Completely fair on both sides.'*

*Bonnie looked around the room. There were three of this man. She knew that this was* the Doctor. *Three of him, but in different forms. He was a shapeshifter too. But not a Zygon. There were two Zygons in the room, corresponding to two females whose forms they were aping. And there was herself. There was her own form. The* Clara *form.*

*This was a significant memory. This was a secret.*

*'So for the next two hours—' interrupted one Doctor—*

*'Until we decide to let you out—' said the second—*

*'No one in this room will be able to remember if they're human—'*

*'Or Zygon.'*

*Bonnie watched as the Doctors wiped the memories of everyone present.*

*This was a cheap trick. A cruel manipulation. A thoughtless erasure of identity.*

Just because you can't remember something, *thought Bonnie,* it doesn't mean that you forget.

*After Clyde died before her, Bonnie made a vow. She would live as herself. She would punish these humans. And she would find this* Doctor *who had condemned her kind to live like cattle. And she would punish him too.*

*She would never forget.*

*She would never forgive.*

## Chapter 12

## The Woman in the Pod

'Hello, good afternoon, you're watching BBC News with Azi Kashani. It's two pm – a summary of the news . . .'

Bonnie watched as the lift descended through the floor of Clara's building She smiled with satisfaction.

'A video supposedly showing an alien in South London is posted across the internet, along with a message warning that there are even more aliens living and working amongst us.

'The Home Office is dismissing it as a fake – urging members of the public not to panic. However, it's quickly going viral. Let's see how Twitter has taken it.'

A few different tweets came up on screen:

*No one seems the same. #WhatTheHellsGoingOn*

*MY MUM ISN'T MY MUM ANY MORE #WhatTheHellsGoingOn*

*AM I GOING CRAZY?????? #WhatTheHellsGoingOn*

The newsreader looked up, blankly and paused. 'Truth or Consequences,' she said.

Bonnie moved along the tunnel, towards the cavern, kicking aside the hairballs of the UNIT detachment. She needed to move quickly. The Doctor was still alive, and Clara was becoming unpredictable; Bonnie needed to accelerate her plan so it could hit full speed before either of them had a chance to stop it.

She moved through the squirming, wriggling pods until she found Clara's.

Bonnie stood and watched it for a moment. Then she closed her eyes.

In her dream apartment, Clara sat in front of her TV. The white noise resolved into an image of Bonnie.

'Hello,' said Bonnie. 'Where is the Osgood Box, and what is it?'

Clara jabbed at the remote, trying to change the channel. It leapt over to another programme: the title sequence to *Strictly Come Dancing*.

But Bonnie broke through again. 'There's no point turning over. There's nothing better on the other side. Unless you like Ant and Dec. Answer my question.'

Clara changed the channel again. She didn't particularly like Ant and Dec, but anything was better than looking at her own evil doppelganger.

The picture jumped back to Bonnie regardless. There was to be no getting away from her.

'I can send you into paralysis,' said Bonnie.

'Then why haven't you?' asked Clara.

She saw Bonnie starting to concentrate, trying to reach the nerve centres of her mind and to put her back to sleep. But Clara was an expert at compartmentalisation, and it was easy just to shut a few doors. *Slam.*

'Gotta do better than that, kid. Having trouble?' Clara smiled. And tried sending out something of her own.

In the Zygon Cavern, Bonnie shimmered into Zygon form, glitching, with a cry of pain. And switched back to human again. This was unexpected. She was losing control. This woman was *strong*, despite her diminutive size.

'This thing goes two ways, you know,' said Clara.

Bonnie set her face. Concentrated. 'Where is the Osgood Box? What is in it? I want those memories!'

'Trouble is, you're asking for them. Which means you can't access them, right?'

'I can *make* you tell me.'

'No, you can't, or you would have already.'

'I can kill you.'

'So do it.'

Bonnie concentrated a moment, sent a stab of pain into Clara's mind. But, a few moments later, Clara sent the same energy back. Bonnie staggered again and morphed briefly.

'I'm calling your bluff,' said Clara. 'You need me alive.'

'Only as a source of information.'

'I'll never share this with you. It's too important,' said Clara. 'Look. We're at a stalemate so why don't we just stop?'

Bonnie stood back and gathered her thoughts for a moment. She needed to change tack. She needed to use this connection. How?

Very deliberately, she placed two fingers on her opposite wrist. She took her own pulse. She smiled.

Clara suddenly felt anxious.

Bonnie looked at her keenly for a moment. 'Our hearts are linked, Clara. Beat for beat.'

Clara took her own pulse, too. Was Bonnie telling the truth?

'The one thing you and I can never do, Clara, is lie to each other. Oops, that scared you, didn't it?'

Clara said nothing. Thinking frantically.

'Answer me. That scared you, didn't it?'

'No!'

Bonnie grinned. 'Yes, it did. Your pulse told me so.'

Clara sat back on her haunches. How was she going to handle this?

'Now here's what we're going to do,' continued Bonnie. 'I'm going to ask you questions. And if you don't tell me the exact and complete truth, I will know and I will kill you. Do you understand me?'

'Yes.'

'I will slaughter you in that pod, right now. Am I lying to you?'

Clara took her own pulse. It was absolutely steady. 'No.'

'Then we'll begin. Where is the Osgood Box?'

Clara stayed silent.

'You will answer me. Truth or consequences: lie and you die. Where is it?'

'UNIT HQ. Under the Tower of London.'

'Where specifically?'

'The Black Archive.'

Bonnie had a flash of the three Doctors, negotiating their pathetic little peace treaty. 'Ah, yes. The dark little storage facility for forbidden alien tech. Who has access to it?'

'The Doctor. He sealed it up after last time. Didn't want UNIT changing their mind about the ceasefire.'

'Does only the Doctor have access?'

Clara didn't reply.

'Ah!' said Bonnie, sensing the minute skip in Clara's pulse. '*You* have access?'

'Yes.'

'How?' Bonnie was starting to find this easier. 'You have a key. Or a pass.' It was becoming more straightforward to intuit Clara's thoughts and feelings from the rhythm of her blood. 'No, a code. A key-code, is that it? Give it to me now.'

Clara gave the faintest smile. 'I can't.'

'Interesting,' said Bonnie. 'You're not lying.'

'No, I'm not.'

'But you have access of some kind.'

'Obviously.'

'So you will give it to me.'

'I told you. I can't. You know I'm not lying. I can't give you access.'

Bonnie closed her eyes and tried to think herself into Clara's thoughts. Into her way of playing the game. 'Okay,' she said, taking things back to first principles. 'How do you get in there? How physically do you get in?'

'A door. It's automatic.'

Bonnie looked at Clara. 'Your body print. Of course, it's keyed to your body print. You can't give me access because I have access already. I'm you.'

'Yes.'

'And what am I going to find? What's in the Osgood Box?'

Clara stayed silent.

'Clara?'

'The box ends the ceasefire.'

'So I'm told. How?'

'There's a button inside the box. Press it, and it will transmit a signal that will unmask every Zygon on the planet.'

Bonnie took this in and smiled. This was exactly what she wanted. This would supercharge *everything*.

'What's to smile about?' asked Clara.

'Mass panic followed by a war. Every Zygon on our

side at a stroke. If they're unmasked, they will have to defend themselves or die.'

'Twenty million Zygons against seven billion humans,' said Clara. 'That's not a war you can win.'

'Then we will die in fire, instead of living a lie.'

'Most of your own kind don't want to die in fire.'

'Then it's time we stopped giving them a choice.'

'No. It's time you asked the most important question.'

'Which is?'

Clara looked at her. Bonnie looked at Clara, and read the response from her mind:

'Why's it called an Osgood Box?' asked Bonnie.

'I'm not telling you,' replied Clara.

'Good. I've been looking forward to hearing you scream.'

'I'm not telling you, because when you get to the Black Archive, you'll find out for yourself. And when you do, you'll want to talk to me again.' Clara was smirking now. 'Am I lying to you?'

Bonnie registered her pulse. Clearly she was not.

'Bye.' Clara picked up the remote and clicked off the TV, severing the link to Bonnie.

'North America reporting back to High Command,' said Kate Stewart's voice.

Bonnie turned. She was slightly unnerved by the mind of Clara Oswald but didn't have time to dwell on it. There in the cavern behind her was a facsimile of

Kate, freshly returned from Truth or Consequences. She was flanked by two Zygon soldiers.

'I'm going to the Black Archive. I'll open it up, you will follow,' said Bonnie.

'Of course.'

'But first, you will locate the Doctor. You will bring him to me.' Bonnie looked at Clara's body, still sleeping, eyes closed, in the pod. 'We need to bring *this* as well.'

The kids sat on the council estate, outside the shopping centre, watching the day unfold in front of them, just as blankly as before. The street-sweeper swept. The hair-balls rustled, and a pigeon crapped on a poster of Michael Bublé.

The Doctor and Osgood pulled up in their van and got out.

'London!' said the Doctor, flinging out his arms. 'What a dump!'

'London's okay,' said Osgood.

'No, it's not, it's a dump.' The Doctor nodded to the kids. 'Hello, strange children. Have you seen my friend?' he asked. The kids ignored the question.

'You spend an awful lot of time here considering it's a dump,' Osgood insisted.

'I spend an awful lot of time being kidnapped, tortured, shot at and exterminated, but it doesn't mean I like it.'

'Well,' said Osgood, giving up, 'this is where Bonnie posted the video from.' They took in the surrounding buildings. The shopping centre sported a faded sign: THE FLEET CENTRE. 'There must be an entry to the Fleet near here,' Osgood mused, looking around. 'Drains? Sewers?'

'Ugh. Why is it always drains or sewers?' the Doctor complained. 'Why can't people hide somewhere *nice*?'

A scream came from the shopping centre. Osgood looked over: a young woman holding a child tore out of one of the shops in front of them, sobbing.

'Shall we go in?' asked Osgood.

'No, leave it. This is a distraction. I'm sick of distractions. We find Clara first.'

'Come on, Doctor. You're not being very Doctorish.'

Osgood walked purposefully through the broken sliding doors of the Fleet Centre. The Doctor clicked his tongue and followed behind. 'I am the Doctor. Therefore, I am Doctorish,' he pointed out.

Osgood didn't reply.

They could feel electricity in the air. Inside the shopping centre, it was dark. It shouldn't have been dark. These were the peak business hours. The lights should have been on and people should have been engaged in the passion of retail. But it was dead.

'It stinks. It smells like . . . barbecues,' said Osgood. A line from *Ghostbusters* crossed their mind: *Barbecued dog hair*.

They turned a corner to find ten or fifteen hairballs, littered around.

'Oh right . . .' said Osgood.

'Close the doors,' said the Doctor. 'Sonic specs setting 87DG.'

Osgood sonicked the doors. The security screens behind them started to descend. The dark darkened and the screens hit the ground with a CLANG. The Doctor took a long, large torch out of his pocket and handed it to Osgood. He took another long, large torch out of the same pocket. They switched their torches on and headed into the heart of the shopping centre, towards the pound shop.

'I'm glad you're not entirely dead, by the way,' said the Doctor.

'Thanks. No. I'm not entirely dead,' Osgood agreed.

'And I'm sorry you lost your sister,' he added.

'I felt it happen. We were linked, all the time. She died and I died with her. Just – not entirely.'

Osgood kept talking, flatly, matter-of-fact. 'I must have screamed for about two days. All the time, just screamed. I wasn't sure that I could ever stop. And then I realised – you don't. You just learn not to scream out loud.'

The Doctor put his hand on their arm, like he understood. 'What's your name?' he asked, softly.

'Osgood.'

'What's your *first* name?'

'What's *your* first name?' Osgood countered.

The Doctor looked at them for a second. 'Basil,' he said.

Osgood looked at him sceptically. 'Petronella.'

'Let's just stick to what we had,' said Basil. 'Look, I need to know something. Because it's important, because it might matter . . . Which one are you? Human or Zygon?'

'It's none of your business,' Osgood replied. Their face was stubborn. They weren't going to tell him.

'I need to know because I don't know what's going to happen,' said the Doctor. 'I don't know what the Zygons are planning. Someone might press a button and you might get killed.'

'I've already been killed,' said Osgood.

'I was happy here,' came a cold voice from the shadows. 'I'm Etoine. I was happy.'

A creature stepped forward from the darkness. Terrified, and terrifying. Half human and half Zygon.

'We're friends,' began the Doctor. 'Etoine, was it? We've come to—'

Etoine rasped at them, raising his hand with a sting already pointing out from it. 'Some people saw me. They attacked me! I had to—' He broke off as a red welt burst painfully across the side of his face. Osgood could see he was trying to hold his human form but slipping back into Zygon. It was clearly agonising. Or perhaps there was something else causing him even more pain.

'I had to kill these people,' he gasped, looking across at the hairballs. 'They were going to kill me. You see, a commander came, *she* did it. She turned me back!' He staggered. Screamed again as his form flitted.

'We can help you,' said Osgood. 'Doctor, we can help him, can't we?'

The Doctor shrugged. 'I'm not sure.'

Etoine turned, glitched a little more and screamed in agony as he stumbled back into the shop and into the shadows.

The Doctor hurried after him. 'Please! Come back! I can't help you just now but, if you help us, we can get you somewhere safe.'

Etoine paused. His form stabilised a little. The Doctor and Osgood slowed as they approached him.

'I can't change,' Etoine moaned. 'I can't hide.'

'Let us help you,' pleaded Osgood.

'I'm not part of your fight. I never wanted to fight anyone, I just wanted to live here. Why can't I just live?'

'We're on your side,' said Osgood.

'This is my home! You've taken my life!' With a yell, Etoine lifted his hands, charging them up. 'Now they'll kill me!'

'No, stop!' the Doctor exclaimed as Etoine gathered together enough force for an electric bolt. 'Don't!'

Etoine rammed his fists against his temples, electrocuting himself. He fell down dead, hairballed.

The Doctor sighed and shook his head.

'Why did they do this to him?' asked Osgood. 'He's not one of the splinter group.'

'No,' said the Doctor. 'He's a refugee who thought he'd found a home. I guess Bonnie thought that made him a traitor.'

'So she unmasked him by force?'

'And he felt cornered enough to defend himself.'

'Doctor, that's what happened in Truth or Consequences. Someone was unmasked. By accident. That's what caused the . . . the riots. That's what started the whole thing . . .'

'I think that's their plan. To unmask everyone – provoke fear, paranoia, provoke a war – make the Zygons defend themselves or die.'

'But, I mean, they could only do it case-by-case. Normalising them by force – it'd take months, years . . .'

The Doctor looked gravely at Osgood and raised his voice.

'If they get to the Osgood Box, they'll be able to unmask every single Zygon in the world. At once. Mass radicalisation in a heartbeat. That's the final sanction. I didn't ever believe that it's something that anyone would *want*.'

'Ah, Doctor,' said Kate Stewart.

Kate and two UNIT soldiers stepped forward through the doors of a lift that led down to the parking garage, and presumably beyond, to the tunnels along the Fleet.

'Kate – you're all right,' said the Doctor softly.

'Of course I am. Why wouldn't I be?'

'I'd heard otherwise.'

Osgood smiled at Kate, but she didn't smile back. She continued, cold and business-like: 'We know where the Zygon command centre is. We know where Clara's pod is . . . We can take you there.'

The Doctor beamed. 'Well. How very convenient. That's just exactly what we're looking for.'

'And here it is. The Black Archive,' said Bonnie. 'Oh, I do like being you, Clara. Everyone just waves you on past.'

This was the locked room in Clara's memory. The dark secret that had been concealed for so long. Beneath the Tower of London, the fortress built by an invader to keep the country safe from invasion. Under the ground, below the robotic ravens whose flesh and blood counterparts had long since fled.

Bonnie inspected the grey metal doors, carved into a stone wall. Behind her were two of her operatives, adorned as UNIT soldiers. Between them was Clara's pod, with Clara still sleeping inside.

'So how does this work?' asked Bonnie, peering at the door. There was a hand scanner set into the wall. She cautiously placed her palm onto the metal plate and it glowed slightly as she pressed her flesh onto it. Locks clanked and moved inside the door. Bonnie grinned at the pod. She was in.

*

Clara watched this on television from her flat, as before. On her face was the tiniest smile.

'Well, as sewers go, it's not so bad,' said the Doctor cheerfully. 'I'm glad I'm a goodie, you know. If you're a baddie, you have to hang about in such smelly places all the time.'

The Doctor, Osgood, Kate and the two UNIT soldiers walked into the Zygon Cavern. The Doctor took in the scene. Hanging pods. He peered up and tried to identify some of the faces half-protruding from inside. He sniffed.

'How many of these things are occupied?'

'We don't know,' replied Kate. 'I did a quick count. There must be at least ten thousand.'

This was every bit as bad as he'd suspected. He recognised a small selection of the great and the powerful, kidnapped and podded. Decision-makers. People who could influence public opinion. People who could control whether or not to go to war.

'I don't know why people bother being baddies, y'know,' he said thoughtfully. 'I suppose it's something to do with their upbringing. But it must be very stressful.'

'Which one is Clara's?' asked Kate.

One of the soldiers let out a low growl. A kind of laugh.

'Doctor,' said Osgood suddenly. 'I think they're Zygons.'

The soldiers normalised. They *were* Zygons.

'Oh, you little tricky monkeys!' said the Doctor.

Bonnie walked into the Black Archive. The lights came on in blocks, illuminating a vast area. It was different to how Clara had remembered it. There was even more alien technology here than there had been three years ago. Think of what she could do with all of this. Think of what she could achieve!

But first, she needed to meet her initial objective.

'Normalise,' said Bonnie.

The two soldiers who had accompanied her with Clara's pod straightened, stiffened, started to dribble and bubble and glow. And then they were Zygons again.

Clara's pod rested against a huge glass case containing items which Bonnie could identify as the head of a Cyberman, the weapon of a Dalek and an Ice Warrior's pencil-sharpener.

Bonnie walked slowly into the room. As she went further, the display cases seemed to thin out. She turned a corner and there, in the middle of a huge, open area was a table. Standing on the table was a large red box. With a big button on top. The Osgood Box.

Bonnie glanced over to Clara's pod, smirking as she moved around the corner and towards the table.

'Well, Clara,' she said. 'I think you're reaching the end of your—'

But as she moved forward, her face fell. Her voice

dried in her throat. There was something there that she had not expected. As she stared in dismay, her communicator squelched. She lifted it to her ear.

'Yes?'

'The Doctor is here,' said Kate over the communicator from the Zygon Cavern.

'Don't kill him. We need him alive.'

'What for?'

'Because I just found out why it's called an Osgood Box.'

Bonnie looked coldly into the open space before her. As well as the red box standing on the table, there was also a blue box, standing at the other end of the table.

'There's two of them.'

'Two Osgoods, two boxes. Operation Double. What did you expect?' said the Doctor over the communicator.

'What's in them? Tell me, now!' screamed Bonnie.

The Doctor didn't hesitate. 'One box normalises all the Zygons.'

'And the other?'

'Destroys them.'

Bonnie moved over to the red box, examining it. 'Which box is which?'

'That would be telling!' said the Doctor.

Bonnie nodded to the two Zygons who had accompanied her. They went to Clara's pod, ripped it open and yanked Clara's limp body from its restraints. Clara woke and came woozily back to life. She looked Bonnie up and down.

'Is that what my bum looks like?' she asked.

Bonnie looked across at Clara and sneered. 'I have Clara here, Doctor. Which box normalises the Zygons? Tell me. Or she dies.'

The Zygon soldiers took up positions on either side of Clara. They each put an arm on her shoulder.

'No. This is war, Zygella. You pull the trigger, you take your chance,' said the Doctor.

'Kill her,' Bonnie barked. The Zygons raised their hands and prepared to sting.

'Blue!' shouted the Doctor.

'Are you lying?'

'The blue one will normalise your people.'

'If you're lying to me, Doctor, she dies.'

'I'm not lying. And you'll know I'm not when you open the box.'

Bonnie took a deep breath. She lifted her hand. Scarcely believing that it could be so simple. She paused for a moment then pressed the button on the blue box. Decisively.

The lid sprang up.

Bonnie leant forward.

Inside the box were two more buttons.

One marked TRUTH and one marked CONSEQUENCES.

'Doctor!' she yelled, her patience at its final end.

She went to the other box. The red box. Recklessly, Bonnie pressed the button on this box too.

The lid shot up. Revealing two more buttons.

One marked TRUTH and one marked CONSEQUENCES.

Bonnie's scream was louder this time. '*Doctor!*'

In the safehouse, the Doctor grinned at the sound of Bonnie's frustration. 'Yeah, I know,' he said, grinning at Osgood, Kate and the two Zygon dudes.

'Bring him to me!' Bonnie commanded over the communicator.

The Zygons advanced on the Doctor. He tensed himself.

Then he heard the gunshot. One of the Zygons collapsed. Another gunshot. And the other Zygon tumbled to the ground. Both were dead.

Kate stood behind them, her gun.

'You're you!' said the Doctor.

'I'm me,' Kate agreed.

'How did you survive?'

'Five rounds rapid,' said Kate. 'One of the best things my father ever taught me.'

The Doctor surveyed the bodies sadly. 'Is that the lot,' he said, 'or are there more Zygons down here?'

'That's the lot, but there are plenty more above ground. They're taking over up there. They're getting ready to fight.' Kate turned to Osgood. 'You are you?'

'I'm me.'

'But Zygon or human?'

'Me,' said Osgood emphatically.

'Okay. Twenty million Zygons about to be unmasked,' said the Doctor. 'They'll be given a choice: fight or die. If they fight, we won't be able to tell who's human and who's not. And you can't kill them, not with soldiers.'

'Which leads me to a very big question,' said Kate.

'I was really hoping it wouldn't.'

'The Z-67. Sullivan's gas, the gas that kills the Zygons. You took it.'

'Yes.'

'That's what's in the red box, yes?' asked Kate.

The Doctor sighed. 'Yes.'

'If I remember rightly,' continued Kate. 'It causes a chain reaction in the atmosphere that would turn every Zygon on Earth inside out.'

'Kate, let me negotiate peace. You can't commit mass murder on that scale.'

'Then why did you leave the gas with us?'

'The boxes are safeguards for both species. They're what you agreed to.'

'I never agreed to that,' said Kate, reloading her gun.

'Yes, you did. Then I wiped your memory. And you agreed to that, too.'

'I'm sorry, Doctor. Truly. But the peace has failed.' Kate raised her gun. 'We need to get to those boxes.'

# Chapter 13

## Truth or Consequences

The Doctor knew what he had to do. He'd done this before. He knew that he had to *perform*.

He knew that, on a good day, there was magic in the way that he spoke. He could make spells and enchant people with his words.

Humans and Zygons were on the verge of a potentially appalling war. What he needed to do was to talk them down. Bring them back from the brink.

That was not going to be easy.

Could he do it? Was it even possible? Could he really change their minds with words and not weapons? Could he encourage empathy in the mind of a stone-cold killer?

The Doctor looked out over the wet London streets as his car threaded its way to the Tower of London and the Black Archive beneath. He would need to be at his very best. He would need to give the performance of his life.

He closed his eyes.

All the greatest performances come from *truth*.

Bonnie stood over the buttons, thinking swiftly, daringly, through her options. Trying to second-guess a Time Lord.

Truth or Consequences or Truth or Consequences?

Which was which? What would be the result? Could she live with the result if she made the wrong choice?

She felt Clara's eyes on her neck and glanced back.

'You're wrong,' said Clara.

'No. I'm right.'

Clara could still sense Bonnie in her mind. There was a lingering telepathic trace. They had each shared something with one another and they had each left something behind.

'What do you want?' she asked Bonnie. Because she couldn't see a fully formed plan there. There was an outline of something in Bonnie's mind but it was clouded by anger and grief and humiliation.

'I want to show humanity who we are,' said Bonnie. 'I want the truth of this to be known.'

'You might not get the war you want,' said Clara. 'Human beings can cope. They can cope with change.'

'They'll be terrified,' said Bonnie. 'Paranoid. If they think aliens are amongst them, if they're not sure who is who and which is which, then all the faultlines'll fracture. Humanity is divided – even without us, humanity is never far from civil war. They won't know who to trust. Not even the people they love most. It will be *chaos*.'

Clara could feel that there was chaos in Bonnie's heart. 'You won't win,' she said.

'I don't care,' said Bonnie. 'I just want the truth to be told.'

'I'm still in your head, Bonnie,' said Clara calmly. 'I'm in your head, and I'm going to change your mind.'

'Hi!' came the voice of the Doctor.

Bonnie jumped. She and Clara turned, and Clara grinned as the Doctor bounded into the light, followed by Kate Stewart and Osgood. The Zygons made ready to attack, but Bonnie stopped them with a gesture.

'Stop this, please,' the Doctor began. 'Let me take both of these boxes away. We'll forgive, we'll forget. And the ceasefire can stand.'

'No,' said Bonnie.

Kate went to the table and stood by the red box. 'Doctor, which of these buttons do I press?' she asked. 'Doctor – which of them? Truth, or Consequences?'

Bonnie stood by the blue box, squaring herself up against Kate. 'Yes, Doctor,' Bonnie said. 'Truth. Or Consequences?'

The Doctor looked at them both for a second. Here they were, Kate and Bonnie, the architects of what would be either peace or war, at the start of the game.

Playing out the scenario – the nightmare scenario. He took a deep breath and began.

'The red box, Kate. One of those buttons will destroy the Zygons. Release the Imbecile's gas.'

(Kate's hand hovered over the box, over the two buttons below.)

'The other one detonates the nuclear warhead under the Black Archive. It'll kill everyone in London and most likely trigger a worldwide nuclear conflict.'

(Kate edged her hand a little further back from the box. The Doctor wouldn't really have rigged something that could destroy his favoured species – surely?)

The Doctor smiled and turned to Bonnie. 'Bonnie. One of your buttons sends a signal that will unmask all of the Zygons in the world. Immediately. Irreversibly.'

(Bonnie looked at him, as if trying to read him.)

'The other cancels their ability to change form. It'll make them human beings for ever. The Zygon race will only ever be a memory – even for yourselves.'

(Bonnie tried to compute what this would mean. Whether she could turn it to any advantage. But she couldn't see a way. She needed to think.)

'There are safeguards beyond safeguards. I negotiated this peace on a very important day for me.' The Doctor remembered: it *had* been an important day for him. It had been the day that he had been saved. A day in which a terrible choice was corrected, a terrible history rewritten. It was the day that he became the Doctor again.

'This ceasefire will stand,' he said.

'This is wrong,' said Bonnie.

The Doctor looked at her. 'No. It's not.'

She looked back sternly, accusingly. 'You have to take responsibility, Doctor. You were the negotiator. You are responsible for all the suffering. All the violence.'

'No,' he insisted, 'I'm not.'

'You engineered this situation. It's your fault,' said Bonnie.

'No, it isn't. It's *your* fault.'

'I had to do what I've done,' said Bonnie.

'No, you didn't,' replied the Doctor.

'We have been treated like *cattle*.'

'So what?'

'We have been left to fend for ourselves,' she hissed.

The Doctor shrugged. 'So is everyone.'

'It's not fair,' said Bonnie.

'Oh! It's not *fair*! Oh dear. I didn't realise it wasn't *fair*! Well, my TARDIS doesn't work properly, and I don't have my own personal tailor,' said the Doctor. 'Is *that* fair?'

'The things don't equate,' snapped Bonnie, her finger poised over one of the buttons.

'These things have happened, Bonnie,' said the Doctor. 'They're facts.'

He came and stood by her. His pale blue eyes were softer now, like a father's or a preacher's. 'You just want cruelty to beget cruelty. That doesn't make you superior to people who were cruel to you, Bonnie. It just makes you a bunch of new cruel people, being cruel to some other people who, in time, will end up being cruel to you. Why don't you break the cycle? I'm sorry for your pain, Bonnie. But the only way anyone can live in peace is if they're prepared to forgive.'

'Why should we forgive?' she asked.

The Doctor hesitated. There had been one moment in his life, a moment that seemed to last for ever, at which he no longer called himself the Doctor, at which he no longer felt entitled to keep that name. He had pressed a button on a box like one of these: the only option open to him to end a war had been to kill everyone, on both sides – his enemies and his own people. He had lived with the consequences of that decision for ever. It had stopped him being who he was.

'What do you actually want?' the Doctor asked matter-of-factly.

Bonnie knew the answer, and she wanted the word to sound strong and powerful.

'*War.*'

But it came out as sad and weak instead.

The Doctor looked at her for a long moment.

'And when the war's over, Bonnie? When you've got

a homeland free from humans, what do you want that to be like?'

Clara searched in Bonnie's mind. The only answer that she could find to the Doctor's question was '*I want to be with Clyde again.*'

Clara frowned. She could feel Bonnie's increasing anger and pain. She didn't know the Doctor's plan. He often liked to provoke people, test their limits, to see how far their self-control went and how dangerous they could be. But she knew that Bonnie was capable of pressing one of those buttons, and she didn't want him to push too far.

Clara tried to reach out, to make contact with whatever part of herself was still in the Zygon's head. She tried to awaken Clara in Bonnie's mind.

'Have you given that future any consideration, Bonnie?' the Doctor continued. ''Cause you're very close to getting what you want. What's it going to be like? Paint me a picture. Are you going to live in houses? You want people to go to work? D'you want people to go on holidays when they're not at work? Are you going to allow music? Do you think people will play violins? Who's going to make the violins? Will there be money? Will people grow potatoes? Will there be enough potatoes to go around? Do Zygons even like potatoes?'

Bonnie gave no answer.

'You see, the fact is, Bonnie, like every other terrified,

tantrumming child in history, you have no idea what you actually want. You know what you want to destroy, you know who you want to kill, you think you know what you want to free people from. But you don't understand what you're freeing them *to*. You don't know what you ultimately want, and that is why you're going to fail.'

Bonnie seemed to think for a moment. Stood a little taller. Her hand hovered.

'The way I see it . . .' said Bonnie, 'it's a fifty per cent chance.'

Kate's hand darted out over her buttons too. 'For us also,' she said.

One race or the other. Genocide.

The Doctor clapped his hands and whirled, seemingly delighted. A crazy, reckless new energy overcoming him.

'And we're off!' he cried. 'Fingers on buttons! Are you ready to play? Who's feeling lucky? Who's quickest? Who's fastest?'

'This is not a *game*!' raged Kate.

'I *know*,' said the Doctor, his craziness dropping suddenly like the mask that it was.

'Then why are you doing this? Why are you acting like this?' demanded Bonnie.

'I'd quite like to know too,' said Kate. 'You set this up – why?'

The Doctor looked at them and said simply: 'Because it's *not a game*, Kate. This is a scale model. Of war. Every war ever fought, right there in front of you. It's always the same. When you fire that first shot, however right and justified you feel, you never know the consequences of those actions. You don't know who's going to die; whose children are going to scream and burn; how many lives will be shattered, how many hearts broken, how much blood will spill . . . until everybody does what they were always going to have to do, from the very beginning.'

Anger ripped out of the Doctor, exploding one word at a time.

'SIT! DOWN! AND! TALK!'

The Doctor's words echoed around the Black Archive, echoing off the dead glass of display cases of devices meant to kill. A silence fell.

The Doctor approached Bonnie. He spoke gently now. 'Listen to me, Bonnie. Just listen, please. I only want you to *think*. Do you know what thinking is? It's a fancy word for changing your mind.'

'I will not change my mind,' said Bonnie.

'Then you'll die stupid. Alternatively, you could step away from that box, walk away from this room, and stand down your revolution.'

'No! I started this, I'm not stopping it. I'm *right*. What they did to us is *wrong*.'

'You can't change it, Bonnie. You can only change the way that you respond.'

'You think they'd let me go now – after what I've done?'

'You're all the same, you screaming kids. *Look at me, I'm unforgivable*. Well, here's the unforeseeable – I forgive you. After all you've done. I forgive the killings. I forgive the violence. I forgive you. If you want the pain to go away, Bonnie, trust me. You need to forgive.'

'You don't understand, you will never understand—'

'I don't *understand*? Are you kidding? Call this a war? This funny little thing? I fought in a bigger war than you will ever know. I did worse things than you could ever imagine. And when I close my eyes –' he said, closing his eyes tightly and feeling the unusual sensation of tears forming hotly under the lids – 'I hear more screams than even I can ever count.'

He took a breath and felt the tears scald his skin. 'And do you know what you do with all that pain? Shall I tell you where you put it? You hold it tight, till it burns your hand, and you say this: no one else will ever have to feel this way. Not on my watch.'

Pain flickered across Kate's face. She stepped back from the box. The Doctor glanced at her.

'Thank you,' he said grimly.

'I'm sorry,' said Kate.

'I know.'

The Doctor looked to Bonnie. Clara felt that the Doctor had jarred something within Bonnie's mind.

'Well?'

Bonnie heard the Doctor's voice. Her head was

bowed: she was staring at the box. When she spoke, her voice was quiet, small.

'It's empty, isn't it?'

'Of course,' he said.

'Both boxes. There's nothing in them, just buttons.'

'Do you know how you know that? Because you've started to think like me.'

Clara closed her eyes. She could feel Bonnie's mind nearby, quivering slightly. Clara summoned up an image of a sad, broken old man who used to be the Doctor. A man who had borne centuries and centuries of pain and been ruined for ever. She sent the image to Bonnie.

Bonnie looked at the Doctor. Their eyes met. She saw a broken old man for a moment, staring back at her. *Don't be like me. Don't do what I have done.*

'Hell, isn't it?' said the Doctor. 'No one should ever have to think like that. And they won't.' He reached for her hands, gripped them in his. Full of love, understanding and compassion. 'Not on our watch.'

Bonnie stared at the Doctor, faintly tearful. There was a catch in her breath.

The Doctor must've heard it. 'Gotcha!'

Bonnie glowered at him – moved but resentful. 'How can you be so sure?'

'Because you have a natural disadvantage, Zygella. I know that face.'

Bonnie looked at Clara, saw the faint smile she gave.

'This is all very well,' said Kate. 'But we know the boxes are empty now. The game has changed.'

'Oh, that's what you've said the last fifteen times,' said the Doctor. With a flourish, he raised his sonic specs and activated the memory device in the ceiling.

Bonnie opened her eyes to find the Doctor watching her. Clara and Osgood were with him. Osgood was tending to Kate, who was slumped asleep at the table. The two Zygons were prostrated on the floor.

'You didn't wipe my memory,' said Bonnie.

'No. Just Kate's. And your little friends' memories, of course. When they wake up, they won't remember what you've done. It'll be our secret. Nobody needs to remember.'

Bonnie stared at him. Still sceptical, still faintly aggressive. She didn't like this game. This wiping of memories, this dictation of terms. This lecturing.

'You're going to protect me?' she asked, incredulous.

'No. You're going to protect yourself,' replied the Doctor. 'I would very much like the two of you to negotiate a new ceasefire. Take all the time you need. I would very much like there to be two species still standing at the end of this.'

'You're one of us now. Whether you like it, or not,' said Osgood.

*

Perhaps Bonnie didn't like it, Clara thought.

'Why are you forgiving me?' said Bonnie. 'I don't understand why you would forgive me.'

Clara remembered why. Eventually, after all those centuries, someone had come out of time and shown the Doctor that there was another way. A way to save the screaming children in his mind. A way for him to forgive himself.

'Because I've been where you are, Bonnie,' said the Doctor. 'There was another box. I was going to press another button. I was going to wipe out all my own kind: man, woman and child. I was so sure I was right. I pressed that button, Bonnie, and I lived with the consequences. But then I got a chance to put it right. I got a chance to change my mind.'

'What happened?' asked Bonnie.

'The same thing that happened to you. I let Clara Oswald inside my head.'

Clara was moved by that. She had sat and talked to that lonely, broken old man on that day in the Black Archive. She had talked to him and changed his mind.

'Trust me,' said the Doctor, glancing at his friend. 'She doesn't leave.'

There was still grief in Bonnie's soul. There was grief for what she had done. There was grief for what had been done to her.

She had felt emotions. Many of these emotions were not Zygon emotions; they were human emotions. The attachment that she had felt for Clyde was deeply human.

The feel of the weak English sun on her face was deeply human.

She had lived too long in this form.

It was time to change.

The UNIT car pulled up outside the school where she had killed the little girls.

Bonnie left the room and walked along the school corridor, looking at the images of the children on the walls. The door to the Zygon Command Centre opened. Bonnie walked in, thinking. Thinking through the terms that she'd negotiated with Osgood. Things would be different now. Things might be better. Things might work out.

Time would tell. Compromises on both sides.

She stood at the Zygon console, started operating the controls, bringing them back to life. She spoke into the command circuit.

'*Zygon High Command. The ceasefire is back in place. You do not need to fight. If you wish to live as yourselves, there may be a way. You are all safe.*'

Bonnie leaned back. Time to stop being Clara. Perhaps time to stop being Bonnie too. She didn't really know who that person was supposed to be. Time for a fresh start.

Her skin bubbled and expanded, and she was a Zygon again.

Clara grabbed her overnight bag from the bathroom in her flat. She locked the door and clattered down the stairs. On the floor below, she could hear Sandeep and his family fixing breakfast. Presumably they were all themselves again and happy.

She walked the short distance down to Dulwich, back to where the TARDIS had been left, beside the playground in Brockwell Park. She felt like she was recovering from a long hangover. It had been wretched to live in that dream for so long.

She felt alive. Felt the sun on her body.

She suddenly thought of Danny. Danny Pink.

She missed him. Danny and Clara.

She sighed. *Bonnie and Clyde.*

Being on Earth reminded her of him. Reminded her of a future which had been suddenly and accidentally taken away. A future that even the Doctor could never take her to.

Perhaps it was time to go with him again. To forget this life for a while and do something crazy and exciting.

Yes. It was time to go with the Doctor again.

One last time.

There he was, with Osgood.

'The TARDIS,' said Osgood.

'The TARDIS,' echoed the Doctor.

Clara looked up at the tall blue box. Osgood and the Doctor stood there admiring it. Clara looked up at it too. It was indeed an object worthy of admiration. It was a loveable thing, even if she and it had not always seen eye to eye.

'What does "TARDIS" stand for?' asked Osgood.

The Doctor looked astonished. 'Surely you know that?'

'Well, I've heard a couple of different versions.'

The Doctor smiled. 'Oh, well, I made it up from the initials, you see. It stands for "Totally And Radically Driving In Space". You wanna come?' he asked. 'All of history, all of the future, and all the universe?'

'More than anything,' said Osgood. And they truly meant it.

The Doctor opened the TARDIS door and raised an inviting, if still disturbing, eyebrow.

'But I think I have to stay,' Osgood added.

'Really? I can have you back a second after you left.'

'You've said that to people before. Right?'

The Doctor shrugged.

'How many of them actually got back a second after they left?'

'Well, there's a first time for everything. I mean, if you insist on it, let's – well, what time is it? – let's – ring the speaking clock – have you got a pen? I'll write it on the back of my hand so I remember. What day is it? Wednesdayish? What year?'

Osgood smiled and shook their head. It wasn't going to happen. 'No, Doctor. I've got a couple of boxes to keep an eye on. And a world to keep safe.'

The Doctor nodded. 'Fair enough.' He looked to Clara. 'What about you?'

'Yeah, maybe,' she said. 'Just this once.' Clara crossed the threshold of the time machine and paused to look back at Osgood as she went. 'Take care, you!'

'You take care of him,' said Osgood. 'Don't let him die or anything.'

'What if he's really annoying?'

'Then, fine.'

'Gotcha' said Clara.

With Clara gone, the Doctor looked intently at Osgood. And Osgood knew what was coming.

'Which one are you?' he asked.

*Why does he keep asking that?*

'Osgood,' they said. With a full stop at the end.

'I have to know.'

*Why?*

The Doctor was getting a bit old, Osgood thought. No. He had got old long ago. Perhaps he was set in his ways. Perhaps his thinking was getting a little stale. That was ungenerous, Osgood said to themself. He probably couldn't help it.

'I'm just Osgood.'

'But human. Or Zygon?' he asked.

Osgood took a deep breath.

'I'll answer that question one day,' they said. 'Do you know what day that will be?'

'The day nobody cares about the answer,' came Osgood's voice – from behind them.

A duffel-coated figure stepped into sight from behind Osgood and pulled down its hood.

It was *another* Osgood.

The Doctor was totally thrown. He stared at the two of them.

'Gotcha!' said both Osgoods.

'Oh, look at his face!' said Osgood.

'It's almost not fair,' said Osgood 2.

The Doctor looked between them, bewildered. 'Buh-but?' he stammered. 'I don't . . . How did you . . .'

'Oh, think it through, Doctor,' said Osgood.

'It wouldn't be right, would it?' said Osgood 2.

'To carry on using Clara's face –' said Osgood.

'– when there's a vacancy,' said Osgood 2.

The penny dropped through the slot in the Doctor's wise old head.

'Zygella?' he whispered.

The two Osgoods corrected him.

'Osgood!'

'But which of you was—'

'Osgood!' they both said firmly. Finally.

'It doesn't matter which of us is which,' said Osgood.

'It only matters that Osgood lives,' said Osgood 2.

'And nothing's going to stop us!' said Osgood.

The Doctor frowned. Then smiled. 'You're a credit to your species, Petronella Osgood.'

'No, Basil,' said Osgood. 'We're a credit to both of them.'

The Doctor, who knew Osgood was only ever a reluctant hugger, nevertheless hugged first Osgood and then Osgood. An exchange of smiles, and the old Time Lord stepped into his TARDIS.

'And you should know,' he said, before he closed the door, 'I'm a very big fan.'

The Doctor was tired. Standing in that room, talking at those people, feeling those feelings once again. It was hard work.

It would soon be time for a change, he felt. A radical change. There were things that he needed to understand. To teach himself. To be taught by others. He needed a new perspective. He'd been much the same kind of man for as long as he could remember. He needed to carry on learning, changing, adapting. That was what he had always done. Glowing dimly somewhere, he saw a future when he might know how Bonnie felt. To be someone totally different. It would be new. It would be exciting. To step away from who he had been.

Clara entered the main area of the TARDIS console room. Stood beside him at the controls of the ship.

'You must've thought I was dead back there,' she said, looking at him. 'At least for a while.'

'Yeah.'

'How was it?'

'Longest month of my life.'

'It wasn't a month. Can only have been a couple of days.'

The Doctor looked at Clara. Dimly, he seemed to perceive the fluttering of black wings at her shoulder. There was not very long left.

'I'll be the judge of Time,' he said.

The Doctor pressed a couple of buttons, and Clara pulled the lever to start the ship.

She liked being in charge of the TARDIS. *I wouldn't mind being the Doctor*, she thought. On the whole, it looked pretty cool.

In Brockwell Park, Osgood and Osgood watched the TARDIS as it faded away. They were not sure that they would ever see the Doctor or Clara again. Within them, they held the memory of what it was like to be Clara. But they could not imagine what it was like to be the Doctor. And perhaps, they thought, that was for the best.

Around them, the park got back to normal. The dust of the Doctor's departure settled.

The sun was shining.

Zygons notwithstanding, this was one of the last truly peaceful years of the twenty-first century.

Osgood turned to themself.

'What next?' they said.

'I don't know. Keeping the peace. Saving the world.'

It sounded like a plan.

'But first, ice creams.'

And the two Osgoods linked arms and walked towards the autumn sun, in hopes of an ice cream van.

## Acknowledgements

I would like to thank Steven Moffat, Brian Minchin, Emily Cook and Rob Shearman, without whom this book would not exist.

I would also like to thank my wife Ragna and my beautiful children, without whom I would not exist.

Peter Harness, May 2023